THROUGH THE FIRE

BY

DARBY WEST

THAT SPECIAL TOUCH, INK

NORTH CAROLINA

ISBN 9780979020049

Printed in the United States

This book is a work of fiction. Any resemblance to any actual person, living or dead is purely coincidental.

I dedicate this book to my children

Charli, Courtney & Brandon

And

My granddaughter,

Makayla

Prelude

My baby brother slept peacefully, his warm body curled into a ball behind the bend in my legs. My parents were arguing in the next room. I looked back at CJ, wondering how he could sleep through all of the shouting. When their voices reached this peak, there was always a fight. I shut my eyes as I heard the lamp crash to the floor and someone falling against the wall. I put the pillow over my head and prayed for morning. It seemed to me that with the dawn of a new day, things that had happened the night before were forgotten. It didn't matter how many sons-of-bitches that they called each other at night, when morning would come their laughter and lovemaking would awaken me. I thought there was not much that separated love and hate.

However, this fight wasn't like the other fights. I heard someone's bare feet running into the kitchen. I heard the clashing of the silverware drawer as it fell to the floor.

"Put it down, Carol Ann!" my father warned angrily.

I got out of the bed quietly and tiptoed into the kitchen. Mommy had a knife! They were staring at each other, both of them breathing heavily.

"I'm tired of you pulling out that knife on me, bitch. You better use it this time, or I'm gonna use it on you!" my father said between clenched teeth.

For a second everything seemed to happen in slow motion. My mother took two steps towards my father, the knife out in front of her. When she stepped back, there was a scream — I don't know who it came from, but my father had a look of surprise on his face as he looked down at his bleeding stomach and then at me. My mother threw the bloody knife into the sink and shook her hands as if they were wet.

"See what you made me do! See what you made me do, Clyde! Why'd you make me do that?" she wailed, falling down beside him and cradling his head in her lap.

I backed out of the kitchen and ran to my bed, pulling the covers over my head. Her wailing filled the apartment, it seeped into all the cracks chasing out the roaches and rats. It continued to wail in my head long after my father was taken to the hospital and my mother to jail.

Miss Anna Mae Johnson, one of the old women in our building came to sit with us. I sat in the floor near the puddle of blood and rocked back and forth, cradling my brown teddy bear in my arms. Tears had long since dried up, and now all I could do was rock and stare, rock and stare. Miss Anna Mae got some ammonia and a sponge and began to clean up the blood from the floor.

"Everything's gonna be alright, yeah be alright," she sang. When she noticed me sitting in the floor she said, "Child, you need to get back to bed."

I didn't want to move, not ever. I wanted the floor to open, to swallow me whole, to take me away. I felt myself being lifted up and carried back to the bed. There was a pain in my chest; a pain that felt like fire. It pierced my soul to the very core. I had to find a way to be able to go about life, to function as little girls were supposed to; playing with dolls, having make believe tea parties, playing dress up; that way no one would notice that I was dying. I didn't want anyone to see that with each passing day my soul was surrendering itself to another life. This was a life where there were no Mommies and Daddies fighting and hurting each other. A life where there was no cussing or men climbing into the window early in the morning to lay with my mother. I wanted a life free from drugs and alcohol. I wanted it so badly; I created it for myself - in my mind. However, the fire burned and burned and it was getting very difficult to pretend anymore, so I stopped. I shut down all functioning mechanisms and just survived.

THROUGH THE FIRE

»CHAPTER 1«

I WAS FOUR YEARS OLD and Harlem was my world; the only world I knew at the time. We lived on the fourth floor of a tenement on 135th Street and Amsterdam Avenue. Our one bedroom apartment was always too cold in the winter, and too hot in the summer. I often sat in the window watching all the activity going on in the streets below. The children in my building were allowed to play outside in the fire hydrant during the summer. Their laughter carried upstairs, so I watched with excitement as they had their fun, wishing I could join them. I knew better than to even ask my mother if I could go outside and play. I asked once and she beat the crap out of me for 'bothering her high', as she put it. In the winter, when it was too cold to go outside the children would play in the hallway. I was allowed to play in the hallway, but only on our floor and the fifth floor where Miss Anna Mae lived. Unfortunately, all of the childhood activity was happening on the floors below mine. I could hear the other children playing handball against the walls, and hopscotch by drawing with a piece of chalk on the black linoleum floor.

They would call up to me, "Come on, Toni. We're not going to tell your junkie Momma!"

I dared not leave my floor and go to play with them. I would shout back down, "My Momma ain't no junkie! Your Momma's the junkie!"

The mean kids would sing a song made up for poor, little knotty haired girls like me. "I know your hair is nappy, but I refuse to lend you my comb if you have to beg and plead for my Dixie Peach, I don't mind 'cause you need it more than me!" This little diddy was sung to the beat of the Temptations' hit, *'Ain't Too Proud to Beg'*. Oh, how I hated those kids!

Harlem was the place to be in the sixties. I thought there was no place like it on earth. Mommy and I would sit in the bay window in the living room on Friday nights and watch as the ladies, decked out in their finest clothes strutted up the street heading to a club or a party.

"I can't believe she squeezed her fat behind in that dress. It looks like if she farts, she would burst right out of it. And look at that ugly fool in that sharkskin suit. If he think he gonna get a woman tonight, my name is Cutie Brown. Listen at him, with his nasty self!" Mommy said.

"Hey, baby. It must be jelly, 'cause jam don't shake like that! Hey Girl, I want to drink your bath water," the men would say.

"Mommy, what is he talking about?" I asked.

"As soon as you get an ass, you'll find out what men like that mean," she answered. The thought of walking down the street and having a man yell out to me frightened me to death. I just wouldn't grow a big behind, I thought.

Right before I turned five years old, my mother had a baby boy. He was named after my father, and we all called him CJ, short for Clyde Jr. I was so glad to have a brother because now I would have someone to play with and I wouldn't have to be around the grown-ups anymore. When they came home from the hospital with the new baby, Daddy let me sit on the couch and hold him. I sat and stared at his butter colored, round face. His head was pointed and the front of his forehead throbbed. He had no teeth and big, hairy ears. His eyes were gray and runny. I was disappointed because I had hoped to have someone to play with right then.

"Don't cry. I know he looks a little funny right now. But in a couple of weeks, he's gonna be as pretty as you were when you were a baby. Don't touch his soft spot," he said pointing to the throbbing forehead. He gave me a bottle of milk to feed him. CJ clasped my finger with all of his, holding on tightly.

"He likes me," I told Daddy.

"He loves you," Daddy said.

By the time CJ learned to crawl, he was getting into all kinds of trouble. I didn't like when Mommy slapped him, or pinched his arms and legs. I just wished he would stay out of trouble. One day when CJ was about ten months old, I was supposed to have been watching him while Mommy cooked some oatmeal for us to eat. It was nearly two in the afternoon and neither of us had eaten yet. It seemed to be taking her forever to cook the oatmeal, so I tiptoed into the kitchen to see what was taking so long. In a matter of a half minute CJ had found her tray of marijuana and had stuffed his mouth with it. He came crawling into the kitchen with a mouthful of leaves and stems. Mommy turned around about the same time I did.

"Boy, what the hell do you have in your mouth?" she shouted.

She grabbed him by his arm and lifted him up off the floor. She slapped him so hard that spit and the marijuana flew across the room. She held him by the arm and continued slapping him until there was no more of her weed in his mouth. CJ was screaming to the top of his lungs. She slapped me across the face very hard.

3

She threw the pot of oatmeal into the sink and turned on the water.

"Toni, how come you ain't watchin' this boy? You greedy, lazy little bastard! Didn't I tell you to watch him? Now neither of you niggers are gonna get anything to eat today. Get outta here!" she screamed.

I lay in the living room floor crying and hurting. CJ crawled in and lay beside me. I looked into his big brown eyes and saw the same frightened look that was most often in my eyes when I looked into the mirror. Mommy came in and threw a bottle of milk in the floor beside CJ. He picked it up and held it tightly. When she walked away cussing under her breath, he tried to put the bottle in my mouth. I drank some of the ice-cold milk, and gave it back to him. When Daddy got home from work, he would have a fit when he saw all of the bruises on CJ and me. He and Mommy would probably argue. He would most likely go out and buy a fish and chips dinner and feed us. Sometimes, it was the idea that he would take care of us when he got home that kept me from crying all day long.

On days when we were very bad, Mommy would lock me and CJ in the bathroom because she knew that big cockroaches lived there and how frightened we both were of them. I would climb into the tub and pull CJ in behind me. Sometimes the milk in his bottle would be so thick that it wouldn't even come out of the nipple. It smelled like cheese. When CJ would start to cry, Miss Anna Mae, who lived right above us would come down and bang on the door.

"Open this door up, Carol Ann! That baby's been crying all mornin'. Open it up 'fore I call Welfare!" Mommy would unlock the door because she knew Miss Anna Mae was crazy enough to do just that; call the folks at Welfare. "Open the door, Toni," she

4

said softly. I would open the bathroom door and stand there crying with snot running into my mouth. "C'mon, babies," Miss Anna Mae would say and take us both upstairs with her. Mommy never tried to stop her.

At Miss Anna Mae's we knew she would give us a nice hot bath, and rub baby oil on us. She always had clothes that nearly fit us that we would put on. She would tie CJ in a chair and help me into one. We would eat a big plate of greens, cornmeal dumplings, fried chicken, and rice with gravy. She wouldn't take us back downstairs until she heard my father coming up the steps. Daddy always whistled when he came into the building. I heard momma tell one of her friend's that he did it so that if she had any men in the apartment, they would have time to climb out of the fire escape before he got to our floor. I believed he did it because he wanted us to know that he was about to rescue us.

CJ and I slept on a fold up bed just outside my parents' room in the hallway. In the morning, the bed was rolled under their bed. Their bedroom was so small that it only had enough room for the bed and a chifferobe. Mommy seldom made her bed. She kept her curtains tied in a knot allowing the breeze to blow in during the summer. The only picture on the wall was the one that was there when we moved in; a white family smiling from ear to ear. All of the walls in the apartment were painted the same ugly, shiny gray color.

My father was a very handsome man, with thick wavy hair and dimples when he smiled. He had a gold-capped tooth that shone like new money. He was soft spoken, but, he didn't take any mess. When my father was angry, his voice would drop to almost a whisper. He would warn a person first that they had better leave him alone. As long as he was yelling, you were good to go, but if he whispered, you had better look out. He worked in the meat district in lower Manhattan. He would leave the house while it was still dark to go to work, and it was dark when he got home as well. He always smelled of smoke; not smoke from fire, but like bacon and hams. He always brought home huge boxes of meat. We had plenty of food to eat back then, just no one to cook it for us. Our freezer was stocked with hams, steaks, pork and veal chops. We had boxes upon boxes of kosher franks and cold cuts.

My mother didn't work because she was a heroin addict. Each morning I would find her sitting in the window waiting for her stash for the day. She couldn't function with it and she couldn't function without it. I watched her go from a woman who was a beautiful golden complexion to an ashy gray. Her large brown eyes were now blood shot and swollen most of the time. White, foamy spit lingered in the corners of her mouth. When I would come to her for food, she would tell me she was too tired to fix anything, she told me to fix it myself. I was five years old and able to scramble eggs and make bacon for my brother and me. My father would come home from work and complain that we had been home all day without anything to eat. I had promised my mother that I wouldn't tell about knowing how to cook. That was to be one of our many secrets, but just like the others, my father found out about this one as well. There would be nothing fixed when he came home for dinner. He would go to the kitchen and cook us a burnt bologna and egg sandwich. He would hold my mother's head up and force her to eat. The heroin was slowly taking her away from us. She lived for the needle and nothing else.

»CHAPTER 2«

WE USED TO HAVE RENT parties to help anyone in our building who was having a hard time paying their rent. One Saturday night all the neighbors had gathered on the third floor to have a rent party for this woman named Sylvia. All the women would get together, cook all kinds of food, and sell plates. The men in the building would supply the liquor and wine. Everyone left their apartment doors opened and the music would be playing throughout the whole building. In most every apartment, a person could get in on a game of poker, smut, spades or dice. The old men would be playing dominoes and checkers for money, as well.

No one ever watched the kids when there were rent parties. We were free to wander from one apartment to another. That's what I was doing when I wandered back to our apartment. It puzzled me that the light was off, but the door was ajar. I stepped inside the dark apartment. I knew where the light switch was, but decided to make my way in the dark, like Spider Man - which happened to be my favorite comic book character at the time. I was tiptoeing down the hallway towards the only light that was on inside my parents' bedroom. Halfway there I heard voices. I eased close to the wall, walking slowly, moving silently. The door was half opened and I could look inside and see the bed clearly.

Mr. Sonny, our new super was sitting on the bed, his back against the wall, naked. My mother was also naked, and was kneeling in

7

front of him. At first, I couldn't make out what she was doing. Then I saw that she had his thing in her mouth! I put my hand to my mouth in shock and disgust. Why in the world would she have his nasty thing in her mouth? I mean, he used it to pee. It stayed closed up in his pants all day long, sweating and smelling. I swore that I would never kiss her in the mouth again, nor would I let her kiss me. She was so nasty!

On the weekends, my father would take me and CJ to Brooklyn to visit his sister Louise, whom we called Aunt Wezie and her husband, Uncle Seymour. They lived in a brownstone in Brooklyn, not far from downtown. It was a beautiful house with lots of rooms and an attic and basement. Since they had no children of their own, they rented out two of their bedrooms to borders. Whenever we went to visit Aunt Wezie she would make me and CJ go down to the basement. I would go, not because I wanted to, nor because I found the basement to be this wonderful place to play, but because it took me away from their talking. Uncle Seymour would be sitting in the basement with headphones on listening to records and drinking scotch. I felt sorry for him because he always looked sad, even when he smiled.

Daddy and Aunt Wezie talked about Mommy.

"Carol Ann ain't hitting on nothing. You need to get rid of her ass. Sorry ho'!" my aunt would say.

My father sat, his head bowed just nodding in agreement. He never took up for Mommy. If he told her how she was so beautiful when she was clean. How she cooked and cleaned the apartment. How she sewed beautiful clothes for CJ and me. How she made crocheted doilies, and baked cookies. All he did was listen and nod in agreement. The reality of it was that everything that Aunt Wezie said was the truth. My dream mother did all of

8

those wonderful things for our family, not the real Mommy. I would sit at the top of the stairs staring down into the basement and wishing that something, anything could quench the fire in my chest.

When my mother was off heroin, our house would be full of men and women. She would cook tons of food for them to eat and open up bottles of my father's liquor to serve them. "I want y'all to stay out of our way. So you better find something to do with that bad-ass brother of yours," she would say to me. CJ and I would both be hungry, not having had anything to eat, but she was more concerned about feeding her friends than us. After they all ate, they would go into the living room. When they got quiet, I knew that they were being nasty. I hated these people because they were disgusting. Sometimes I peeked into the living room to see naked men and women doing it to each other. Even the women would be with each other, and my mother would be right in the midst of them all, with her nasty self. Before it was time for my father to come home, they would all leave. She would open the window to let some fresh air in and straighten up.

"Y'all eat some of this leftover food," she would order before going to the bathroom to shower.

There was never any leftover food, except what was in their plates, picked and messed over. We would be so hungry, we didn't even care that the chicken bone we were nibbling had been in someone else's mouth, or that we were drinking out of someone else's glass. Our mother certainly didn't care either, since she was the one with the big idea.

Sometimes the grown-ups would ask me to dance for them. I loved to dance. They would clap their hands and cheer me on, laughing. "Shake your money maker, little momma!" the men would shout. Afterwards they would give me a dime or a quarter. Some of them would offer me a sip of their drink. I would take it because I had to obey. The scotch would burn my nose and throat as it went down. I would gag, tears welling up in my eyes. For some reason the adults thought it was funny. Some of the women, though, might hug me, which was okay. I was able to fit in; to have someone like me - if but for a brief moment in time.

Paul was in the Army. I don't know where Mommy met him, but all of a sudden, there he was. He was tall, very dark chocolate and wore his hair in a process. He always had a doo-rag on to hold it down. He walked around my father's house like it was his own, with just his green army pants, and a tight t-shirt. He would come to our house very early in the morning and stay there all day long. Mommy told me to call him "Uncle Paul", but not to mention him to Daddy or my nosy aunts. From my parent's bedroom I watched silently as Uncle Paul and Mommy slowed danced across the floor, kissing. He would talk to her, holding her tenderly. She began to fix her hair. She put on makeup and dresses. She stopped getting high when she met Uncle Paul. I could tell when they were about to "do it" because she always made me go out into the hallway to play, and threatened to beat the crap out of me if I came inside before she called for me.

I was sitting in the floor under the kitchen table one day while they were making plans. "I can make you happy baby. I'm fixin' to go to Germany for four years. I want you with me. Tell me you'll come with me," he said quietly waiting for her answer.

"You know I'm gonna go with you, Paul. I love you!" she said.

They made plans for their trip. I listened, yet never heard her say one word about me and CJ. She was going to leave us and go all the way to Germany; wherever that was - with this man who had

10

come into her life and taken my father's place. I hated her and wished that she was dead. Yet, I loved her and wanted her to stay. I ran to her one afternoon and fell against her breasts. I don't know what it was that possessed me that day, but I was there begging her to hug me back. I looked into her eyes and saw nothing.

She pushed me away and yelled, "Stop acting like a baby. Get your ass on! Get! I said. Get the hell on!"

I stepped back frightened. Uncle Paul was sitting next to her, looking at my mother in shock. I stared at her, frowning. I couldn't understand how she could love him, hug and kiss him, yet she couldn't feel the same for me - her child.

"Did you hear me, you little bastard. You best to get out of here," she hissed in my face.

Her tone scared me nearly to death.

I turned and ran from the room and went into a corner. It was dark and cold there, yet warmer than in my mother's arms. I huddled there crying silently. "Why did you talk to her like that? She just wanted you to hug her," Uncle Paul said. He got up and came to me, pulling me to him and apologizing for my mother. "She loves you, you hear. She does," he said so convincingly.

I looked at him, "She does?" I asked. He nodded his head yes.

"I love you too," he said.

Then his lips were on mine, my father never kissed me on the lips like this. His lips parted and I felt his tongue in my mouth. I tried to pull away, but he held the back of my head. When he was finished, he pulled away and got up, joining my mother. I knew the kiss was wrong. Grown-ups are the only ones who were supposed to kiss like that. I tried to avoid him from then on, but he always seemed to be able to get me alone. He would touch me in places that I knew to be wrong.

"I've been real nice to you, girl so you better not tell nobody 'bout me. I don't want to have to hurt you," he warned me, a strange look in his eyes.

I would disappear when he was there. I hated Uncle Paul, but I hated my mother even more for allowing him to hang around our house all of the time with his nasty self.

»CHAPTER 3«

"MISS ANNA MAE, CAN YOU watch the kids while I run to the A&P?" my mother asked one day.

Miss Anna Mae let us in, and CJ ran to play with the other kids. I could feel that something was wrong. It was time! They were going to Germany! It hit me in an instant. I ran to the window looking out. I saw them put a small suitcase in the back seat then they get into his shiny black car.

"Mommy, please don't leave!" I screamed out silently. "Don't leave us!"

We were at Miss Anna Mae's for a long time. She would go down stairs and check to see if Mommy had come back home. I knew in my heart that I would never see her again.

When we heard Daddy coming up the stairs whistling '(Sitting on the) Dock of the Bay', Miss Anna Mae went in the hallway to talk to him. I wanted to sneak to the door and listen, but I didn't really want to hear that she was gone. The door opened and Daddy and Miss Anna Mae stepped inside. He was smiling, but his eyes were sad.

"Hey, how's my babies?" he asked.

"I don't know how any mother can up and leave these two precious babies for some skinny, little nigger that ain't hitting on nuttin!" Miss Anna Mae said.

13

Daddy cut his eye at Miss Anna Mae and she stopped talking. We ran to Daddy and hugged him tightly. When we got downstairs, I went to their bedroom and looked in the chiffarobe. Some of her clothes were still there, but the little plaid suitcase was gone.

It was Friday so Daddy didn't have to work the next day. I didn't want to be around Miss Anna Mae to hear her talk badly about my mother. Daddy let me and CJ lay in their bed that night. CJ went to sleep as soon as his head hit the pillow. I lay awake listening to my father calling people in Mommy's family to see if anyone had heard from her. If anyone had, they certainly weren't telling him. I cried and sobbed loudly because I was convinced that she left because of something that I had done. Suppose she found out that Uncle Paul was kissing me and rubbing his hand between my legs. Suppose she would have stayed if I had watched CJ better, or stayed out of her way when she had company. It had to be something that I did to make her want to leave us. Daddy heard me crying and came to stand in the doorway.

"Let tonight be the only night you cry over that bitch, you hear? Tomorrow you better not shed one tear for her. She ain't worth it no way," he said before walking away.

His words cut like a knife. I lay awake for a long time before sleep finally took over.

"Toni, hold your brother's hand," Daddy said.

I took CJ's hand and walked down the stairs to sit on the stoop. I knew that my father was trying to convince Miss Sarah to let us stay with her. When we sat down CJ laid his head in my lap. We were both very tired. It seemed like we had not gotten much sleep since Mommy left us. As the midday sun beat down on us, I prayed that we would go home soon. I was so tired of riding

14

around in the car, watching Daddy beg these women to let us stay with them. We went to probably fifteen different houses that Saturday, but none of the women he visited wanted to take care of us while he was at work. Some of the women didn't even open the door when Daddy knocked and a few of them cussed him out. However, most of them were nice enough to answer the door. He let us either wait in the hallway, or we went inside and waited in the kitchen while he begged, buttered up, and tried to coo these women into watching us until he "got his ducks in a row," whatever that meant.

Around two in the morning, not having had anything to eat since breakfast, he pulled up in front of our building. He carried CJ up the four flights of stairs to our apartment, and held my hand pulling me along. If he hadn't I probably would have fallen down and slept right in the stairway, I was so sleepy. He pulled out the trundle from under his bed so that we could lie down to go to sleep. From his bedroom, I heard him praying and crying quietly.

"Father, you've got to help me with this situation. I'm lost, Lord. I'm lost. I can't make it without you, Father. Please help me find a place for my babies. Just for a little while. I pray this in Jesus' name. Amen," he said.

I didn't understand why he didn't just call Aunt Wezie. She was married, had a big eleven-room house, and no children. She would have let me and CJ stay with her. However, that idea didn't seem to come to my father, and I was too young to suggest it. Then too, his other sister, Luciana lived in the Bronx in a three bedroom apartment with just her two kids. She sure would have taken us in, if she knew that he was riding around New York City begging his old girlfriends to watch us while he got his ducks in a row. I sat in the car handing him nickels to put into the pay phone as he started calling the rest of the names in his book. He

15

was good at begging, but everyone seemed to be turning him down. He told me that he needed to find someone before that night; this was Sunday morning. Finally, he got a woman that agreed to watch us. He skipped to the car grinning from ear to ear.

"You gonna like your Aunt Liz. She's real sweet. Loves kids! That she does. Yeah, you're gonna love her," he said happily.

I glanced at CJ. He looked scared. He had also used the bathroom on himself. I laid him in the seat, took a diaper out of his bag, and changed him.

"Throw that thing out the window!" Daddy said when the smell hit his nose. He was in a good mood now.

»CHAPTER 4«

DADDY LIED BECAUSE AUNT LIZ was not sweet. She didn't love kids; and we didn't love her. Oh, she was sweet when she was talking to my father.

"I'll keep them until Friday. But, you have to give me forty dollars. That covers three meals a day. I wouldn't charge so much but that boy ain't potty trained. And if I got to be cooking for these kids, I need to be paid extra for it, cause I ain't a domestic! They had better do what I say, and stay out of my way when I'm working. Do you hear me, man?" she asked him in a serious tone, since he was standing there grinning so.

"Yeah, woman, I hear you. They're good kids. And my daughter knows how to cook already and clean. Don't you Toni?" he said to me.

"Why you name that girl Tony?" asked Aunt Liz.

"Her real name is Antoinette, silly!" Daddy answered her.

He pulled Aunt Liz to him and gave her a kiss on the lips.

"Hey, wait a minute. I don't give away free kisses! And speaking of money, I want twenty of it up front!" she said pushing him away.

Daddy took his wallet out and took out a twenty.

17

"Here you go. And you better take good care of them," he warned her.

He bent down and gave both me and CJ a sloppy kiss and left. We stood there, scared to death while this Aunt Liz person returned our stare.

"What you know how to cook, girl?'" she asked.

"I know how to make bacon and eggs," I said quietly.

"Well, you little niggers look hungry. Go fix yourself some food," she said.

We followed her into the kitchen and she sat down at the table. I put CJ in a chair and went to the sink. I couldn't reach it.

"Do you have a stool?" I asked her.

"Naw, but I got a bucket if you just needing something to stand on," she said.

She slid a large aluminum bucket out from behind the table and I stood on it while I cooked bacon and eggs. She talked the whole time I was cooking. I was thinking to myself that if I do a good job, she will fall in love with me and my brother. She'll let us stay with her not just for one week, but forever. She'll want to be our mother and take care of us.

"Girl, I hope you know you're sorry ass momma ain't hitting on diddly. Any woman that up and leave her kids ain't worth spit. I know that I won't be a good mother, so I don't ever want none. I'm too mean and selfish. Besides you little niggers always be needing sum'in. Y'all be needing shoes, and clothes. And this little snotty nose nigger smell like he needs to get his behind washed. I'm gonna change him this time, but I be doggone if I'm gonna be changing crap off some sorry man's child. You hear me, *Toni*?" she said, over emphasizing my name.

She took CJ to another room and was gone for a while. When she came back, he was clean, and dressed in an oversized pink silk t-shirt. "This here is my good luck t-shirt. I hope that this little man will bring me a real man 'fore long," she said. She got down some plates and I fixed all of us a big plate of food. "Girl, you can cook!" she said, "Look at you!" she added surprised.

After we ate, she told us to go into the living room and watch television, because she had to get ready for work. When she shut the door, I got down from the couch and looked out of the window. There was another row of buildings just like the one we were in across the street. Kids played outside, darting in between the parked cars to catch a ball or run to the next base as they played stickball. Aretha Franklin singing Respect blasted from a tape player while teenagers danced on the sidewalk. I wondered if we were still in Harlem or Brooklyn, or perhaps the Bronx. We could have been on Staten Island, for all I knew. And where did she work dressed like she was in a see thru nightgown? I found out real quick as the men entered and exited her apartment most of the night.

Around ten, Aunt Liz came into the living room and told me to help her get the couch ready so we could go to bed. "Men make me sick! That nigger didn't want to give me but ten dollars. I told his behind to pay up, or get out. I swear to God!" she fumed.

I had no idea what she was talking about, but I listened quietly. I had learned this game from the days when Mommy would have people over, and they would pick me to have grown up conversations with. All you had to do was act like you were interested, and that you knew what they were saying by nodding and mumbling huh- uh.

19

"When you grow up, don't you let no man run over you, you hear. Tell them what they want to hear - you know. Tell them they're fine. Can't nobody do it like them. Hell, tell them you love them too. It might get you a few dollars, but girl, don't fall in love. It ain't worth it. That's how I ended up in this mess I'm in," she said.

We had taken the pillows off the couch, pulled out the sleeper, put sheets on it and got blankets down from the closet. All the while, she gave me this bit of schooling.

"Y'all sleep good, ya' hear" she said on her way out of the room.

CJ had used up nearly all of his cloth diapers. Being I was responsible for him, and since I couldn't get to sleep, I thought I would get up and rinse his soiled diapers out in the bathtub. I got the plastic bag that held them all and went to the bathroom. I ran some water in the tub and knelt down with a bar of Ivory soap to begin to wash them. Aunt Liz entered the bathroom dressed in the weirdest outfit that I had ever seen on a person before. I learned later that it was a garter belt and stockings. She came into the bathroom, smiled wearily in my direction and began to run some water in the face bowl. She reached behind the toilet, got a bottle of vinegar, and poured some into the water she was running into a red plastic bag. She put one leg up on the lid of the toilet and began to wash her vagina with a soapy washcloth. From my sitting position down on the floor, I could look up at her and see her brains. I thought that adults were the grossest people in the world; and I silently hoped and prayed that I would grow up to be a bit normal. After she finished washing herself, she took the plastic bottle, hung it on a clothes hanger over the shower rod, and sat down on the toilet with a white tube sticking out of her. *Do you not see me sitting here? Am I invisible?* I wanted to shout at her.

20

THROUGH THE FIRE

Things weren't all that bad at Aunt Liz's house though. At first she tried to act like she didn't like us, but I could tell she did. She was very concerned about cleanliness. Each night we took a bubble bath. I had never in my life taken a bubble bath. After I dried off, she would sniff my underarms and butt to make sure I was clean. She gave me toilet water to put on. "One dab behind the knees drives a man crazy!" she would laugh as she dabbed some behind my ears, and knees. I silently hoped that no man would be coming up behind my knees.

Aunt Liz enrolled me in school around the block from her house. Even though I hadn't gone to kindergarten, I knew how to read and could keep up with the other children.

Aunt Liz didn't like my hair, which was nearly to my waist and wild. I was tender-headed and cried when she even so much as came in my direction with a comb. Therefore, one Saturday morning, she announced that she was taking me to get my hair done at a beauty parlor. I had never been to a beauty parlor before. As we walked down the block people who were sitting out on the stoop would holler out to Aunt Liz. It seemed that she knew everyone in the neighborhood.

"Where are we?" I asked her. She looked down at me and laughed.

"Poor thing, don't even know where you are. Ain't that a blimp!" she said.

She never did say where we were, I had to figure it out on my own. I saw many trucks unloading and loading up meat just like in lower Manhattan where Daddy worked, but I could tell by the rundown buildings that we were not in the city. I looked up at the street sign as we waited for the light to change. It read Hunts

21

Point Boulevard. I found out a few weeks later that we were living in the Bronx.

I sat in the big black chair while Aunt Liz and the beautician clucked over me.

"Huh-uh! No! You better not cut one strand of my baby's hair. I want you to give her a wash and press. Put some of them Shirley Temple curls up in there. And you better not burn her!" she added, winking at me.

"You gonna be so fine, baby girl!" I smiled.

She called me her baby!

Every Friday my father would come by to give Aunt Liz her money. Sometimes he would come while we were still up. If he did, he would take us with him back to Harlem. Our old apartment was the same as it was when our mother left. She still had clothes hanging in the chifferobe. Once I asked Daddy if she was coming back.

He looked at me and replied, "Baby girl, your mammy is gone. Gone, bye. Just left. Adios. And don't mention that ho' to me ever again! You got that?"

I nodded my head yes. And she was indeed history. The only time that she ever was mentioned was when someone would take the time to tell me what a slut she was, ask me how she could leave her kids, or to remind me of all the wonderful things that they are doing, and that she wasn't doing anything. The latter was done more often than I wanted to hear, more often than I could count. It got so I didn't want to go to Harlem with Daddy anymore. He began to send Aunt Liz a money order for us through the mail and he stayed away.

THROUGH THE FIRE

Aunt Liz was a prostitute, but not by her standards, since she didn't walk the streets. She told me that she was a woman of the evening. She was a beautiful woman who loved to laugh and play with us. She and I would look through her photo albums. She told me that she was raised on a cotton farm in South Carolina.

"I saw what the fields did to my Mama, and I'd be doggone if I was going to grow old before my time. I ain't but twenty-one years old, and I will never be a day older," she would add laughing.

The fire in my chest was slowly subsiding. I would sit next to her on the stool in front of her vanity and watch as she put on her make-up. She had freckles on her cheeks and nose. However, by the time that she finished putting on her make-up you couldn't even see them. With precision, she drew a line with the liquid eyeliner across her lids and filled in a mole beside her lips. She always wore red lipstick and finished it all off with a dusting of face powder.

"Let somebody tell me that I don't look good tonight, girl, I believe that I just might have to cut 'em!" she laughed.

One day, after nearly a year my father showed up and said he found us another home. I had already started first grade and school was almost over. I loved going to school and loved my teachers and classmates, so I didn't want to leave. I could hear him and Aunt Liz fussing.

"How you sound? You just gonna waltz up in here and take these babies. They been here over a year, Clyde," she argued.

"If you think I'm gonna leave my kids with a hooker, you're a bigger fool than I thought!" he yelled back.

23

"Oh my hooking ass was good enough for them when you didn't have anybody else. I was good enough for them when they sorry mammy up and left!" she screamed back at him.

For a while, they went back and forth. Unfortunately, Daddy won out. CJ and I were sitting in her living room. CJ was coloring and I was pretending to be reading a Spiderman comic book.

"Your Daddy came for you, Toni," she said quietly. "Help me get your stuff together," she said.

I felt it in my chest first as it tumbled repeatedly causing me to gasp for air. The tears burned my face, hot and wet. Aunt Liz stepped towards me pulling me to her. I buried my face against her chest surprised to hear her heart pounding. I pulled back puzzled because she had felt the fire too.

"It's not gonna be so bad at your new home. Your Daddy loves this woman and says they gonna get married. See, it ain't so bad," she whispered.

We packed our things up silently. My father sat in the living room talking to CJ. When we were finished, Aunt Liz sat down on the bed across from me.

"Let me tell you something. Don't you let anybody run over you. You have to be strong for you and your baby brother. If you ain't happy at this house, you call me. Don't let nobody sell you no wooden nickels," she said.

We hugged again and then joined Daddy and CJ by the door.

My father let us sit up front with him. He talked a mile a minute because he was so excited. He told me that six and a half months ago he was coming home on the JFK Expressway and began to have a bad nosebleed. He was rushed to the hospital where he met the woman who saved his life. Well, she was the woman who assisted the doctor who saved his live, or at least helped to stop his nose from bleeding. From that moment on, he was smitten. Her name was Barbara Littlejohn and he wanted us to meet her. He told me that he had arranged for us to stay with her mother who lived a few blocks away because Barbara was having their house remodeled. When we got to our new grandmother's house, a large brick and white shuttered house in Queens, I knew that anyone who lived so wonderfully had to be a wonderful person. Barbara's mother and I clicked immediately. Her name was Antoinette D. Carson.

"You stop letting people shorten your name. Your parents named you Antoinette and that is what you should be called," she told me.

From that day until about five years later, I was Antoinette.

»CHAPTER 5«

CJ AND I MOVED IN WITH Grandma Carson that very night. At Grandma Carson's CJ and I had our own bedroom. I had mine at one end of a long pined hallway, and CJ's was next door to hers. She chose it that way, so that she could get up in the night and take him to potty. However, CJ was so used to sleeping with me that he would come to my room and get in my bed. The first couple of times Grandma Carson tried to make him go back to his room but, he would pitch such a fit that she left him alone.

Grandma Carson was nice to me and CJ but she had so many rules it made me dizzy. For instance, as our feet hit the floor in the morning we had to make our bed. We weren't allowed to wear our pajamas in any other room of the house, just the bedroom. So, after making the bed we had to dress for the day. We brushed our teeth and washed our face before we could eat breakfast. During the week, we ate the same thing for breakfast; either Cream of Wheat or Shredded Wheat, depending on the weather. On the weekends, we were allowed to have a big breakfast - anything we wanted. Unfortunately, we couldn't think of anything, except bacon and eggs, since that was the only breakfast food that we knew of. Grandma Carson got tired of fixing us the same thing week after week so she began to cook what she wanted.

My first taste of a waffle with powdered sugar and maple syrup, and many skinny little sausages was dynamite! Pancakes! Grits and home fries! Buttermilk biscuits with strawberry preserves!

THROUGH THE FIRE

It was all too much for a young child to behold. CJ and I would eat so much that we both would be sick the entire day - until dinnertime. When we lived with Mommy we had to eat Daddy's cooking most of the time - and that left nothing to be desired. When we lived with Aunt Liz, most of our meals were takeout dinners. At Grandma Carson's we were getting fried chicken, baked ham, brisket! She served all kinds of fresh vegetables - greens, cabbage, squash and beans! Well, we went from being stick thin, to two fat little children. Yeah, we got plenty to eat. We had nice clothes, and a nice place to live, but there was no one to love us. The only time she hugged us was when we had spent the weekend at Barbara's and came back home.

I was given fancy porcelain dolls, but was not allowed to play with them. I had real china tea sets, but couldn't take them down from the shelves that they sat on collecting dust. Grandma Carson didn't think that little girls should wear pants unless it was very, very cold outside. So, I had very frilly and fancy dresses, and matching silk panties. If I squat down in the floor, she would nearly go into cardiac arrest. There were no games that I could play at her house that would warrant me having to be in the floor with my panties showing. Because she didn't believe that little girls should wear pants, if I went outside to play, I had to remember that I had on a dress, and if I got wild, everyone could see my bloomers. Therefore, I sat on the stoop watching the other children having fun. I knew better than to get up and join them because every so often Grandma Carson would come to the door to check and make sure I was still on the stoop. It was such an awful way to tease a child. I was seven years old, and had never played with other children. I had spent the first years of my life entirely with grownups. All I knew was grown-up problems and grown-up fun.

27

Two years after we moved to Queens I awoke one night to find CJ down at the foot of the bed. I think not having him in the crook of my legs is what woke me. He was crying softly and holding his stomach. When I touched his forehead, he was hot and sweaty. I ran to get Grandma Carson. She took his wet pajamas off and held him in her arms. His big brown eyes were full of fright; and he whimpered as if he were in such pain.

"Antoinette, call Barbara and your father and tell them to get over here right away," she ordered.

Grandma Carson and I watched as they sped away to the hospital carrying him in a large stripe sheet. She fixed a pot of tea and carried it into the parlor on a silver tray. She poured a cup for me and I sat in the floor at her feet sipping it. I was so afraid for CJ. I knew he must be very scared at the hospital without me. I started crying and Grandma Carson held me in her lap for a minute.

"He's gonna be alright," she kept saying over and over.

I must have fallen asleep, because I woke up in my bedroom, tucked tightly under the covers. I could hear crying from the parlor. My father was rocking back and forth and crying loudly.

"Where's CJ?" I asked frightened.

Barbara ran and put her arms around me and led me to where my father was.

"Daddy, where's CJ?" I asked again.

He just shook his head and kept crying. I knew that something terrible had happened. *What is going on?* I wanted to scream.

"Honey, they did all they could. He died," Barbara said.

28

THROUGH THE FIRE

I looked at her.

"You're a liar! You're a liar," I screamed.

I ran through the house calling for my brother.

"CJ! CJ!" I called out.

I hoped he was playing a game of hide and seek. "CJ!" I kept calling, but deep down inside I knew Barbara was telling the truth. That awful fire burned worse than it ever had. Now I was all alone. First, I lost my mother and now my brother.

We had to dress up to go the funeral home. When I saw CJ lying in the tiny, white satin coffin with his Easter suit on, he looked like he was just asleep. I touched his face, and it was cold and rubber and I drew back my hand quickly.

"How's he going to breathe when they close the top?" I remember asking Daddy.

"He'll be o.k. when he gets to heaven," he said. That night and many more after that I had nightmares about CJ.

All day long things were going on around me. I got up each morning, made my bed, and dressed. I washed my face and took the roller out of my bang. I put lotion on my face, and put my tiny pearl earrings in my ears. I went down stairs where Grandma Carson gave me a bowl of Cream of Wheat and orange juice. I got my coat and walked the five blocks to school. The other children in the neighborhood tried to be friendly to me, but I didn't want to be bothered. None of the teachers or children said much to me after a while. In the afternoons, I sat staring at the television set watching Batman and Spiderman. I could hear people around me talking, and sometimes I would answer them. The pain in my heart, the emptiness I felt would not go away. It

29

burned so intensely that I knew the only way to cope was to just go about the motions, pretending that everything was just fine.

While we were out of school for Spring break our math teacher, Mrs. Clarke moved away and our new teacher was named Mrs. Bonner. By the end of the first day, she noticed that I kept to myself and said nothing to anyone. When we were at lunch the next day, she came and sat with me.

"Hello, Antoinette," she said.

I bit into my liverwurst sandwich and chewed it slowly, so I didn't have to answer her.

"I used to be just like you when I was a child. But, you know the best way to make a friend is to be a friend. See those little girls over there at that table? Tomorrow I want you to go and sit with them," she said.

I turned to look at the girls at the table. They smiled and waved to me. I knew who they were because they all lived in my neighborhood. I guessed that I could do that, I certainly was willing to try since Mrs. Bonner had asked so nicely.

I missed CJ so very much. No one had explained to me about death, so I thought he had left me just like my mother had left. I was afraid because so many people had been in my life and now were gone. What kind of person was I that caused people not to want to be around me? I tried so hard to please Grandma Carson. I was always asking her to let me do something for her. I didn't mind taking out the trash, mopping the kitchen on my hands and knees, or vacuuming the entire house. I wanted to make her happy, so happy that she would never want to leave me, or have me leave her. Working so hard after coming home from school would make me tired at night. However, as soon as I lay down, I would start to think about CJ and the fact that he was closed up in a coffin that had been lowered into the ground. I thought that he was probably a ghost now, and if he was he probably would come back to mess with me since I didn't go with him to the hospital. I would ask Grandma Carson to let me sleep with her, but she didn't think that children should sleep with adults. As a compromise, she would let me keep the light on in the hallway. Yet each movement, every shadow was CJ's ghost. I cried myself to sleep each night until I figured out what I needed. I needed to feel that after my long, fretful days, there had to be peace within the darkness. I began to sleep with a pillow balled up behind my legs. Soon all was well with the darkness.

My father married Barbara in the winter and I moved into their home several blocks from where Grandma Carson lived. Here I go again, I thought to myself. We lived in a large white house, with black shutters on the windows and a big black door with thick glass. I had my own room again, and complete access to the basement. I loved the basement. It was finished in dark pine just like at Grandma Carson's. One entire wall was covered with thick mirror glass.

The wood beams that I thought held up the house were located in the middle of the basement, right in front of the mirrors. I would pretend to be a ballerina. One day Barbara saw me dancing and enrolled me into dance class. For the next five years, I studied jazz, tap, African interpretation and ballet.

Things were going good at Barbara's house. I had a beautiful home to stay in. In my bedroom, I had my own record and eight-track player. On Saturday mornings, my friends and I went to the Marcus Garvey Recreation Center on Jamaica Avenue for our dance classes. We played house in Maria's backyard, using her eleven-year-old brother, Manny as the father, me as the mother.

31

I would pretend to cook meals on the brick barbeque grill. I would open bags of Sugar Babies candy and miniature size pieces of Tootsie Rolls and put them in a pot together, pretending it was beans and franks. All of us had plenty of Thumbelina dolls, so we would swap clothes, and sometimes the dolls themselves.

A girl that lived up the block developed a brain tumor. Her name was Dorothy. When she came back to school wearing a wig, the mean boys snatched it off her head on the home one day and threw it back and forth, making her cry.

"Give her wig back", we yelled at them.

Maria was the only one of us who was crazy enough to hit one of the boys. When he hit her back, we all jumped on him beating him to the ground. His so-called friends ran off leaving him to us. After that, Dorothy tried to make sure that we were nearby before she would walk home from school. I felt sorry for her because I knew that she would probably die, so I was extra nice to her. She died around Memorial Day, right before our block party. I remember Mommy asking me if I wanted to go with her to the funeral. I had been to one funeral in my life, and that was more than enough for me. I did make a card to give her mother, though.

The years passed quickly when I lived with Barbara. I worked very hard around the house, washing dishes, cooking breakfast, cleaning all the bathrooms and even working in the flower garden. I didn't want to move again, so once again I was willing to do whatever it took to stay there. Before I knew it, I was in the fifth grade. Because I did my chores, I got an allowance, so I was able to go to the movies on Saturday mornings, or ride the train to Delancey Street and shop for some of my own clothes. Life was finally good to me. I seldom noticed the pain in my chest now.

THROUGH THE FIRE

When I was twelve years old, Barbara suggested I have a sleepover in the basement. I had three close friends that I wanted to invite. Camille and I had lived on the same block since I had moved over here to live with Daddy and Barbara. Maria and Doreen were about three blocks away. We had been friends since that day in the third grade when Mrs. Bonner made me sit with them for lunch.

I was so excited about having all of my friends come over and stay the entire night. Barbara and I went shopping for snacks the night before the sleepover.

"You can get anything you like," she said.

I had never had a sleepover, nor had I been to one, so I didn't know what you did at one, or what you ate. Barbara began to fill up the shopping cart with ice cream, sprinkles, chocolate syrup, nuts and other stuff to make sundaes. We got packages of Jiffy Pop Popcorn, Bugles and Oreo cookies. When we walked in the house with four bags of goodies, Daddy shook his head and went to the den. The basement had recently become his domain since he had purchased a pool table. He was not too thrilled to hear that he wasn't going to spend Friday night in the basement drinking beer and eating pickled pig feet with his friends from work. I could hardly wait for the girls to arrive that Friday evening. Each time the doorbell rang, I squealed with delight. By 7:30, all of my friends had arrived. We danced around in the basement lip singing to the Supremes' latest songs until we were out of breath from laughing so hard.

"Let's make some sandwiches," I said taking the girls upstairs.

To our surprise, there was a large platter of sandwiches cut into cute little shapes on a big platter in the middle of the dining room table.

33

"Thanks, Barbara!" I said and kissed her on the cheek.

When we had gotten back to the basement, Camille asked me why I didn't call Barbara "Mommy."

"I don't know," I said. I had never thought about it before.

"You should. I mean she does everything for you like a real mother does. She's really the joint. I would call her Mommy if I were you. After all, she has been your Mom since we moved to Queens," Maria said.

They were right. Barbara did act like a real mother is supposed to. There was no reason why I shouldn't call her Mommy. I wanted to check with Daddy first, though. I was able to talk to him about it that Sunday morning while he was in the den reading the paper and waiting for breakfast.

"Daddy, do you mind if I call Barbara, Mommy?" I asked.

He didn't act surprised. He put the paper in his lap and looked at me for a few seconds. I was nervous, my palms sweating.

"Say something!" I said.

"Well, baby. That's really up to you. Barbara has been a mother to you. I know she loves you very much. If you really want to make her happy, that would do it. She can't have kids of her own since the operation."

"What kind of operation?" I asked concerned.

"She had a tumor down there and now she can't have kids," he explained.

I felt just awful for Barbara. I called Camille immediately to tell her what Daddy had said.

THROUGH THE FIRE

"Barbara had a tumor down there and had to have an operation. She can't have children now," I told her.

"Oh my goodness, Toni! You really need to call her Mommy now", she exclaimed.

»CHAPTER 6«

ONE HOT SUMMER DAY WHILE I was at Camille's house sitting out in her backyard talking, I felt this sticky moistness in my panties. I stood up to see that my white shorts were now bloodstained. I started to scream. My first thought was that I had cut my privates. Camille was staring at the stained shorts, eyes bucked. I ran into Camille's house and locked myself in her bathroom. I removed the shorts and my panties and washed my body. I looked under the cabinet and got one of Camille's mother's pads. Camille pushed me a clean pair of panties under the door. I put them on, and waited while she found me some shorts to wear. I rinsed out my own clothes in the sink and wrapped them in a plastic bag.

Back at home, Mommy came into my bedroom carrying a box of Kotex, some Midol pills and a Macy's bag containing several pair of black panties.

"If you wear black panties it would be better. That way you can't tell if they are still stained after they've been washed. You need to mark this date on your calendar. And...," she rattled on.

I was only twelve years old. It was way too much information to retain. I remembered only the important things - write the date on the calendar, keep some Kotex and Midol handy, and wear black panties.

The second month I got my period, I also began to experience severe cramps. I had never felt anything that intense in my life. I couldn't even walk when I had these cramps. I also would have a high fever, chills, diarrhea and vomiting. Mommy took me to several doctors who told her that my symptoms were in my head. They told her that I was experiencing such a trauma from having my period at such a young age, that I was literally making myself sick! However, everyone in the house knew that I was not making this up, I was sick!

My father just didn't know how to handle this. He would come into my room and sit gingerly on the corner of the bed, while I moaned and groaned and rolled around thrashing. I had to keep a bucket near the bed to throw up in. I couldn't even drink water.

"Try some of this," he offered one day.

It was some hot ginger tea. I felt about five minutes of relief and then threw it up.

"Here baby, try this," he said later on.

It was a shot of whiskey with lemon and honey in it. I had taken many shot glasses of this mixture when I had colds.

"Are you sure this works on cramps?" I asked looking him in the eye. He was smiling.

"Yeah, it works on everything," he said.

I gulped the whiskey and laid back. He was and reading the newspaper to me when my stomach began to churn and I sprayed him and the whole paper with bitter vomit. After that, they let me lie in the bed, thrashing in pain and crying alone. The only good thing about the whole experience is that the cramps only lasted the first day of my period.

DARBY WEST

I became interested in boys when I turned fourteen. I was shy around them, but I had this crush on this one particular boy named Melvin. He was a grade ahead of me, but he had flunked Algebra and was taking it with me. I was thrilled to be able to just sit two rows over from him. The only person that knew that I liked Melvin was Camille. I would compose long, boring poems about my "undying" love for Melvin and read them to Camille every day after class.

"I'm so sick you and Melvin. Girl, he doesn't even know you exist. He's not going to ever know either, unless you say something to him!" she told me one afternoon.

"Oh Camille, you know I can't tell him. He might not like me," I said.

"Girl, tomorrow, I'm telling him," she stated.

"No! Oh, please don't tell him. Please don't. I will die!" I begged.

All the next day, in Algebra class I would look at Camille with this begging, pleading look in my eyes. She would pretend that she was writing a note and going to pass it to Melvin. I would put my hands up in a begging gesture, pleading silently. She would lick out her tongue. This was the longest hour of my life! When the class was over, and Melvin had safely walked out, I collapsed on the desk. Camille had a big laugh about it. That ended my crush on Melvin.

During the summer vacation, something remarkable began to happen to my body. My breasts, which use to be little hard knots, were now full and I thought they were beautiful. I had a very small waistline and my hips were developing. I looked like the sexy models in the magazines, or so I thought. I wore hot pants all summer long. My hair, the wild mass of stuff I used to pull back into a ponytail, I now wanted straightened.

My father didn't like the way I dressed and so he came home one Saturday afternoon and laid a shopping bag from Macy's on my bed while I was out. There were several pairs of Bermuda shorts in the bag! He didn't like the fact that I was no longer wearing my hair in a ponytail, but down in curls. If he could stop it, I would never have grown up. Camille and I were both very filled out. We just thought we were the hottest things walking the face of the earth. We brought each issue of Essence and Cosmopolitan magazine, and sneaked on makeup when no one was watching. We would take the train to the city and walk up and down Broadway or go to the Village and check out the sights. Even though Camille and I were always talking about boys, neither of us was interested in actually having sex. Maria and Doreen, however, were already sexually active. They could only describe it as "okay", which wasn't enough for Camille and me to defy our very strict parents and try it. Also, neither of us had a boyfriend yet. On top of that, there were at least one hundred girls in our school who were pregnant.

Before school started the next term, Maria was pregnant. The four of us cried together when Maria told us that her parents were sending her to live with her grandmother in Puerto Rico. A few weeks after she left Doreen found out that, she was pregnant too. She left to go upstate to a school for pregnant girls. It was just Camille and me.

Every time we turned around our parents was giving us that speech about waiting until we got married, or my father's favorite one, "Do you want to end up like that crazy ass woman I married the first time?"

DARBY WEST

I was sixteen when Camille and I found out that Coney Island was the place to hang out during the summer. With our allowance we would take the train there early in the morning. We rode every ride, flirted with the cute people and ate Nathan's franks until we were sick of them. My favorite ride was the Himalayas because it always played the latest jam. The Himalayas was similar to a roller coaster, but smaller and closer to the ground. I would go on this ride all day long. It was at Coney Island that I saw the finest man I had ever laid eyes on.

The chemistry that we shared was unbelievable. I knew from the first time that I saw him that we would be together forever. Even though I was sixteen, I was very shy around guys. He was seven years older.

"Can I buy you a Coke?" he asked.

I had just gotten off the Himalayas and was very dizzy. I leaned against him for a second, feeling his arms around my waist.

When I caught my breath, I replied, "Yes."

He held my hand and smiled as we walked to the boardwalk together. It was 1975, and in the background, Marvin Gaye's "Let's Get It On" was playing.

"What's your name?" he asked showing the whitest teeth I had ever seen on anyone.

"Toni, short for Antoinette, and this is my friend, Camille," I said.

"It's nice to meet you, Camille. Toni? I like that. You look like a Toni. My name is Michael. Do you believe in fairy tales?" he asked.

"Yeah, I do. Why?"

"Because I am your knight in shining armor and you are going to be my princess. My wife," he said smiling.

"Oh is that a fact?" I asked.

"Yes, my wife. Don't tell me you didn't feel it?" he said.

I took a long sip of my Coke and nodded my head yes. We spent the afternoon talking and walking along the beach.

"It's getting late. I told my parents that I would be back home by eight. It was nice meeting you. Can I give you my phone number?" I said.

"Do you have to leave now? It's only six thirty," he asked.

"Yeah, I do. I have to take two trains and a bus to get home," I said.

"I've got a car. Let me drive you. I won't hurt you," he added after seeing me hesitate.

I looked at Camille. She nodded that it was fine with her so, we stayed until seven thirty. He drove a beat up Chevy Impala that needed a new muffler, but I didn't care.

"Can I come and see you tomorrow?" he asked when he walked us to my door.

"No, I'll meet you somewhere. I'll call you," I said.

He leaned down to kiss me, but I went inside my house quickly. I had only kissed one boy my entire life. He was my age, and neither of us knew what we were doing. Michael was different; he was a man. I didn't want him to know how inexperienced I was.

41

»CHAPTER 7«

CAMILLE AND I LAY IN bed that night talking about Michael. He made me feel so special, so warm. I took the piece of paper that he had written his number on and called him. It was way after eleven and no one answered the phone. I was very disappointed. I finally dozed off around midnight. I floated through the next day. He told me that I should wait and call him after six, when he got home from work. I wanted to meet him somewhere but he said that something had come up suddenly, but that he would call me in a couple of days.

We talked on the phone for nearly an hour. The next day I met him in front of the Brooklyn Academy of Music. I was wearing a peach shorts outfit with white laced sandals. I had a peach scarf tied around my hair. Michael wore bell-bottom jeans and a polo shirt. He was so skinny, I could see the print of his ribs though his shirt. I remembered thinking, I have to get him home with me and let Mommy fix him one of her wonderful meals.

We got some Chinese food to go and went to the Botanical Gardens in his beat up car. The flowers were in full bloom. After we ate, we walked around. He was very quiet. I was frightened thinking he had changed his mind about me.

"I've got something to tell you about myself," he said as he led me to a bench.

I could hear my heart pounding in my chest. "I've got two children, by two different women. My son Brian lives in

Baltimore with his mother and her husband. He's seven years old. My son Remy lives in Brooklyn with his mother, Tina and her mother. She and I live just a few apartment buildings apart. Tina is still in love with me. She gets upset whenever she knows that I am interested in someone else. I don't want her to come between us," he said. He looked so worried that I quickly reached out and put my arm around his neck.

"I don't care about that. I only know that I want to spend my entire life with you. And no one or nothing can come between us," I said.

He looked at me a moment and then he kissed me. He pulled away and laughed softly.

"C'mon, girl!" he said, taking my hand as we ran through the park laughing.

We had been seeing each other about three weeks before I decided I had better tell my parents. I told Mommy first. She and I had grown very close.

"Mommy, I love him so much. He is tall, and handsome. He has the biggest, brownest eyes and thick black lashes. He has a beard like Teddy Pendergrass and he is gorgeous, Mommy." I said as we lay on the bed talking.

"A beard? How old is this boy?" she asked.

"He's not a boy, Mommy. He's twenty-three. That's not too old, is it?" I asked her.

"No, that's not too old. Your father is ten years older than I am," she reminded me.

43

Daddy, on the other hand didn't take it so kindly. "I would like to meet him," he said.

I knew that Daddy would have a fit if he knew that Michael had two children by two different women. He would've had a fit if he knew he had one child. I couldn't tell him that right now, and I made Mommy promise that she wouldn't say anything until after he had a chance to meet him.

Unfortunately, when the opportunity arose for Daddy and Michael to meet, Michael messed up, it was a Saturday night and he told me that he had made reservations to take me to dinner at Horn of Plenty. This was such a big night for us. I had gotten my hair pressed for this event. I was wearing a black spaghetti strapped dress with black sling backs. Michael was supposed to pick me up at seven. I was ready and waiting. However, seven came and went, so did seven-thirty, eight and then nine. It had taken him a month to get reservations. I couldn't believe this was happening. I didn't want to sit down because my dress would wrinkle up. I had been standing this whole time. When I called his house, his brother said that he left four hours ago. I didn't know what had happened to him. I was close to tears, but I refused to cry because the tears would smear my eye shadow. Mommy came into my room at nine-thirty.

"Honey, he's not coming. Why don't you take the dress off and get ready for bed," she said softly.

"Mommy, how could he do this to me?" I cried falling across my bed. She put my head in her lap and smoothed my hair.

"Honey, maybe something happened," she said, but I could tell that she was upset also.

Later that night, as I lay in bed I could hear her and Daddy fussing. "I told you in the beginning Barbara, that I didn't think she should be seeing him, but you wouldn't listen. I knew that he would hurt her. He's irresponsible," Daddy said.

"He's not irresponsible. He has a full-time job, and a part-time job. He's taking care of his two boys," and then she stopped. I turned my head towards their door quickly to hear what Daddy's next response would be.

"What?" he nearly screamed.

"Calm down, Clyde. Everybody makes mistakes," she said.

"That's it! I forbid her to see that man, now you hear me. I forbid her to see him!" he shouted. I put my pillow over my head and cried myself to sleep. I had to continue to see him. I just had to!

At eight the next morning the phone rang. Michael had been at the hospital all night because his youngest son, Remy had an appendicitis attack and had to have an operation. I was so sorry for all of the terrible things that I had been thinking about him.

"Can I meet you at your place?" I asked him.

"Yeah," he said.

I quickly got dressed. After scribbling a note to my parents, I sneaked out of the house and took the train to Crown Heights. He was obviously tired. He let me in and led me down the hallway and to his bedroom. His brother slept peacefully on the pullout sofa bed with a girl also asleep at the opposite end. Michael had a waterbed.

"Lay down," he invited, but I was afraid. I sat in a chair.

45

"Girl, I am not going to bother you. I'm too tired," he added, smiling. I went to the bed and took off my shoes. It was like being in a raft. I gingerly lay down and turned on my side facing him. He was grinning. He leaned over, kissed me gently on the lips, and closed his eyes. In a few minutes he was breathing softly, sound asleep. I too fell asleep.

When I woke up it was way past two in the afternoon. I got up as quickly as I could and tiptoed into the living room. I had to call Mommy and let her know where I was. There was a woman sitting in the kitchen drinking soda and eating pizza with Michael's brother, Brian.

"Hi, may I use the phone?" I asked.

I called my house and Michael's brother and his friend fell silent, eavesdropping.

"Hi Mommy, it's me," I said.

She told me that she didn't mean to tell Daddy about Michael's sons. Then she told me to come home.

"I will when Michael wakes up," I said. She gasped.

"No, Mommy we didn't have sex. We just took a nap," I assured her.

I could see that the two at the table were listening to my conversation by the way they smiled and made eyes at each other when I told Mommy that Michael and I hadn't slept together.

"Thanks for letting me use the phone," I said.

The woman stood and faced me.

46

"I'm Tina, Remy's mother," she said.

I know the surprised showed on my face, I didn't have a chance to snatch it back. I took her outstretched hand and shook it. I turned and went back into Michael's room. He was waking up.

"Hey, did you sleep, or did you watch me sleep?" he asked.

"I slept. I just met Remy's mother," I said.

"Oh, she's still here?" he said. There was no surprise or any kind of expression on his face. I sat down in the chair and put my shoes on.

"I'm going to leave now. I'll call you later," I was annoyed, but he didn't even notice.

I walked back into the living room. Michael's brother and Tina were standing in the vestibule laughing and whispering. They both turned and looked at me at the same time.

"I'm going home now. It was nice meeting you," I lied.

They backed up against the wall making room for me to pass between them. I shut the door quietly behind me but I heard them both burst out laughing. I could taste the saltiness in my mouth from holding back my tears. I walked up the block heading to the train station. Then I saw Michael and Tina leaving out of the building holding hands, and laughing. They didn't even see me when they drove past me.

I didn't call him back that day as I had told him. In fact, I tried to block him out of my mind, but after a week I couldn't resist, I called him.

"Hi there, I have missed me some you. Where have you been?" he asked.
47

"I was thinking... I was thinking that maybe we shouldn't see each other anymore. You've got so much stuff going on in your life, and all," I said.

"Girl, don't you do this to me. I told you that I plan on marrying you one day and making you my wife," he said softly.

"It's just that I wasn't expecting Tina to be at your house, and then she laughed at me. I just don't want to get hurt and everything," I said.

"I would never hurt you. I will never hurt you," he promised. I went to his house that day.

We looked at old movies on television and ate popcorn. He drank a couple of cans of beer. He took me home around nine that night. It was very nice, very comforting being with Michael. We just did "friend" things. I did things with him that I could have done with one of my girlfriends. He didn't even try to kiss me, let alone anything else. Well, he kissed me on the cheek, when it was time for me to go, but that was all. He would drive me to the corner of my block and let me off. I still hadn't told my parents that I was still seeing him. I guess I had been sneaking around seeing Michael for nearly six months. We very seldom kissed or touched each other, except to hold hands. It was starting to get to me. I thought perhaps that I didn't appeal to him, so I asked him. He laughed and pulled me to him.

"Girl, trust me! You get to me. That is why I don't kiss you. I know that you are a virgin and that is the way that I want you to remain. Now if I start kissing on you and we both get excited, well... you won't be a virgin for long. Okay? So, don't think that you are not appealing," he said.

Then he added that it was time for him to take me home. I was very disappointed. I wanted him to want me, to make some kind of advance towards me. All of my friends were doing it. I just didn't understand.

One Saturday night Michael and I were going to go to a party at one of his frat brother's apartment. I had been to a few parties before, but only with kids my own age. This was going to be an all-adult party. It took me a while to decide what to wear. I didn't think that I should wear a pair of jeans and a tank top, and wasn't sure if I could get out of the house with a dress and heels on either. I decided to wear jeans, and pack a dress to change at Camille's house.

"You look real good, Toni. I can't tell that you're not an adult," she assured me.

I did look much older, sexy even. It was drizzling, so I put on a raincoat, which also hid my outfit from Camille's parents.

It was our plan for me to take the train to his apartment, and go to the party from there. Brian let me in and told me to have a seat while he went to get Michael. I sat down in the living room, my hands resting in my lap. I could hear muffled laughter and talking, but had no idea where it was coming from. After sitting there about fifteen or twenty minutes, Tina came into the living room. She had on a pair of men's boxer shorts, and just a bra.

"Hi," she said gaily.

She had an empty glass in her hand and took it into the kitchen. She walked back through the living room and then I heard a door close. More laughter and talking followed. What was she doing over here? I wanted to get up and leave, but I was too mad. After another twenty minutes or so, Michael came into the living room

49

wearing some boxer shorts, no shirt. He was surprised to see me.

"How long have you been here?" he asked as he bent to kiss me on the cheek.

"I've been here nearly an hour! What is she doing here?" I asked not even caring how loud I was talking.

"Let me get some clothes on and we can leave. I wish you had let me know that you were here," he said.

"Your brother was supposed to tell you that," I snapped.

He glanced back quickly, puzzled by my anger, but kept on going down the hallway.

After another half hour, he came out dressed. He took my hand and pulled me up from the sofa.

"I am really sorry. I had no idea you were here. I spoke to my brother about it. We still cool?" he asked, bending to my height.

I nodded my head and walked out the door in front of him. We stood waiting for the elevator in silence. I stood there with my arms folded across my chest. I was sick of this situation, but didn't want to give him up. He seemed to need me. He told me that so often that I was beginning to believe it, so I put up with the hurt and said nothing.

When we got to the brownstone that his friend lived in, the music was so loud that I could hear it thumping in my chest from down the block where we had to park. As we got closer, it was worst. There had to be a hundred or more people there. They were packed into the first two rooms like sardines. There was no furniture in either of the rooms, just the stereo and these huge speakers. Danny, his frat brother, spotted him and came over. After giving each other this long and drawn out handshake, they hugged and laughed uproariously.

Danny turned to me, "So, this is the precious cargo. Man she is fine!" he said. "You did well," he added.

I felt like a picture, a piece of art, not his girlfriend, and to make matters worse I was petrified to be there. The smoke from cigarettes and marijuana was thick in the air. I clutched his hand tightly until my knuckles were numb.

Every time that he took a step, I took one. I was on him like white on rice. We danced, but were barely moving because there wasn't that much room. Many guys were looking at me, but it was quite obvious that I was with Michael.

He told me, "Every man in here is checking you out, girl. But you are mine!"

As the night wore on, the party began to thin out somewhat. By three that morning, there were about fifty people left. A lot of them were necking and petting openly. Michael was talking to one of his friends on the right of him. I was standing on his left. Less than two feet from me was a couple kissing and petting. I didn't mean to stare or anything, but I had never in my entire life seen anyone kiss like that. I got embarrassed and turned away. Michael and I soon wandered off into another part of the house, it could have been a bedroom, except the only piece of furniture there was an extra-large beanbag chair. I sat down on the chair and he sat down in front of me. He was smiling at me, his eyes glazed over. I think that he must have smoked a joint or something. I could smell it the room, on our clothing, and in his hair. I probably had a contact high. He started laughing, shook his head and walked to the window. I got up and followed him.

"What's so funny?" I asked.

"I want you so much. I want you," he whispered and pulled me to him.

He released me, took my hand, led me back to the chair, and sat down in front of me. He stroked my lips with his index finger and then he kissed me. He had kissed me before, but not a French kiss. I could hardly breathe I was so excited. I could feel his hands on my thighs.

He pulled away, "Take these off," he said heavily, referring to my pantyhose.

The vinyl was cool against my body. The red light in the room made everything appear to be in slow motion. He eased my dress up and spread my legs. I had no idea what he was going to do. Then I felt his tongue on my thighs, cool and wet. I closed my eyes and touched his head. He spread my legs more and then I felt him kissing me there. Oh my, I loved this man! I wanted him to make love to me. I felt this feeling in the pit of my stomach and I just wanted to scream. I held him so tightly and then he moved away, laying his head in my lap.

"Please Michael make love to me," I begged.

He shook his head, "C'mon, let's go. It's late," he said.

I put my hose back on with trembling hands. He helped me pull them up around my hips. He was kissing me and holding me.

"I'm sorry," he whispered in my ear as we stood there holding each other.

When I sneaked into the house that morning, it was nearly six. No one was up. I undressed and lay under the covers. I got my diary from under the mattress and wrote down everything that happened that night. I wanted Michael so much. He wanted to wait. He said he wanted to marry a virgin. He had told me that so many times, but I didn't know if I could wait. I wondered if he were having sex with Tina. I suspected that he was since she was always there, but I wanted to be sure. I picked up the phone and called him. He had just walked into the house.

"Are you having sex with anyone?" I asked.

He chuckled at first, stalling. Then realizing that I was serious, he asked me what prompted me to ask that question. I told him that I was just thinking of him and trying to figure out why he didn't want me.

After a moment he said, "Yes, I am. I have to have it. However, that doesn't mean that I don't love you. These other women don't mean anything to me," he said.

"Are you sleeping with Tina?" I asked.

Again, he paused, and then he finally said "Yes."

I hung up the phone, angrily and cried into my pillow. Okay, I could half-way understand that he had to have sex. I couldn't understand why picked her to sleep with. He knew that she loved him, and each time he slept with her, made her think that he loved her also. I called him back. He picked up the phone on the first ring. "I don't want you to sleep with her anymore," I said.

"Okay. I promise," he said simply.

Being just sixteen years old, and silly I believed him.

When I woke up Mommy was standing over me yelling. She knew that I came home at six. She had smelled my clothes, and smelled the marijuana in my clothes. She assumed that I too had been smoking. I tried to explain, but she was screaming so loudly. I put the pillow over my head to drown out the sound of her voice. My father wasn't home. He would kill me if he heard what she was saying. She didn't even allow me a chance to explain. She mopped around the house all that day, not speaking to me. I decided that I would go to a movie, yet she refused to let me out of the house. I stormed out anyway. Halfway down the block, I heard her yell, "Don't come back tonight."

What was her problem, I wondered.

»CHAPTER 8«

CAMILLE AND I WENT TO A movie, the mall and then to White Castle's. I went to her house afterwards and we lay across her bed talking. It was nearly eleven thirty. I had school tomorrow.

I called home but Mommy wouldn't let me get a word in she just repeated her earlier statement, "Don't bother to come home."

I told her to put Daddy on the phone. I went home anyway, going to my room. I went directly to my room and got ready for bed. She came in and sat down on the side of the bed.

"Are you still seeing that Michael person? Your father and I forbade it!" she said.

"Mommy, I told you that I had to see him. I love him. I want to be with him," I pleaded.

"Never, ever again," she said.

She left the room and turned off the light on her way out. Michael and I continued to see each other. I just tried very hard to be careful that my behavior didn't give me away. Michael couldn't call me at home, or come over. We had to meet at his house or somewhere else.

Somehow, through all of this sneaking around to be with him, I managed to keep my grades up so during my senior year of school, I had only needed one credit to graduate. I took that class at two o'clock in the afternoon. To fill the rest of my day, I decided to get a job. This also allowed me time to spend with Michael. My journalism teacher helped me get a job at the New York Post as a receptionist. On my way home from school one afternoon, I could hear my father's voice half way down the block. He had never raised his voice to Mommy that way.

"If she calls while I'm here, I'm gonna tell her just what I think of her sorry ass. I swear Baby, she better not call while I am in this house!" said quietly.

I knew he was mad then.

"Hello!" I called out loudly to let them know I was home.

I had no idea who they were talking about. Daddy stood up and went to the basement, slamming the door behind him angrily. Mommy mumbled a hello and went to her room slamming the door behind her too. I sighed loudly and went to my room, slamming the door. An hour later Mommy knocked softly and came in. She had been crying and she looked very concerned.

Toni, your birth mother called here this morning. She's living in Brooklyn at an Army base with her husband and two children. She called because she wants to see you. That's why Clyde is upset. I told him that I thought you were old enough to decide for yourself whether you want to talk to her. Anyway, she's supposed to call back at five to talk to you. If you don't want to talk to her, you don't have to," she said.

My mind was totally blown. She's in New York. She has other kids? Why does she want to see me now? It's been twelve years! Did she know that CJ had died?

All of these questions ran through my mind. However, no words came from my lips. I simply nodded when Mommy was telling me all of this.

She patted my leg, "If you want to talk about it, I'm here for you," she said.

I could only nod okay. She walked out the room shutting the door behind her.

I sat on the bed, cradling my knees against my chest. I tiptoed into the hallway to call Camille.

"Do you want to see if I can stay over tonight?" she asked.

"Please…" I whispered through the tears. Camille was there in thirty minutes.

Mommy was taking a pan of Shake-n-Bake pork chops out of the oven. She went to the basement door and called for Daddy.

"I ain't hungry!" he said.

Mommy, Camille and I sat down to the table to eat dinner.

"How's school?" Mommy asked Camille.

"It's okay. I don't like geometry much," she answered.

"Do you like the rice, Toni?" Mommy asked me.

"Yeah, it's different," I said.

57

Other than that, no one said a word. After dinner, I volunteered to do the dishes and she went back to her room, shutting the door. I was angry that this woman, who hadn't been in my life in over twelve years, could call and stir up this much mess in my home. I hadn't seen her since I was five years old when she lied and said she was going to the A&P and never came back. Mommy said that she had other kids. I wondered how many and how old they were. Why didn't she give them away like she had done me and CJ? Why didn't she send for me when she got herself together? How come she didn't send a card or write a letter? Why, after all of this time did she want to talk to me now?

"Do you see how angry your Dad got? That's probably the reason why she didn't try before, or for all you know, maybe she did call before. Maybe she's even wrote letters. You don't know. I think you should see her. Check out the husband and the kids. She might treat them just like she treated you. You don't know, Toni. Just see!" Camille said.

Three times that night the phone rang. One was a wrong number. Aunt Lucille called and then at ten o'clock just when we had all given up she called. Daddy was asleep. Mommy answered the phone. She came into the den where Camille and I were watching Saturday Night Live. I picked up the phone hesitantly, watching Camille.

"Hello?" I said.

"Antoinette!" she said in a husky voice. "How are you, baby?" she asked.

THROUGH THE FIRE

The last time I heard that voice, was when she lied and said, *"Watch these two for me please, Miss Anna Mae. I have to run to the A&P. I'll be back in an hour."* She abandoned us, went off to Germany, and never looked back until now.

"I'm not a baby anymore. I'm seventeen," I said

"Yeah, you're all grown up. Do you still have all that thick hair?" she asked.

I wiped a hot tear from my cheek. "Yes, I still have long hair," I said.

"I have two daughters now. You have two sisters," she said nervously.

I couldn't think of anything nice to say. I couldn't care one way or the other that she had other children. I didn't know them. I didn't feel any sisterly feelings towards them. I remained silent.

"I was hoping that you could meet them this weekend. We're going to have a cook out. Would you like to come? We would love it if you could," said asked.

I looked at Camille. She nodded her head yes. "Ask her if you could bring a friend?" she whispered.

"I'll come if I can bring a friend," I said.

"A boy?" she asked.

"No! A girl!" I snapped.

She would think it would be a boy! She wanted to come and pick me up, but I knew that if she came to the house Daddy would probably shoot her.

"No, I'll come out there. Just give me the address," I said.

When I told Daddy about it the next day, he walked out of the room and went to the basement. I went down to talk to him.

"Daddy, I know you're still angry about what she did. I am too. But, I have to see her. I have things to ask her that no one else can answer," I said.

"Like what?" he asked looking directly into my eyes, piercing my soul.

"Like why did she leave like she did? Why she didn't stay in touch with us…"

"I can answer those questions. She ain't no good. She's a whore. She's scum of the frigging earth!" he snapped. I knelt in front of him and held his hands.

"I've got to do this, Daddy," I said quietly.

His eyes were bulging and I could hear him breathing. His chest heaved. Tears rolled down my cheeks. We sat there staring at each other. Slowly his breathing relaxed. His eyes softened and tears rolled down his face. He hugged me.

"I just don't want you to get hurt again. That's all baby. I can't let her hurt you again," he said

On Saturday morning, Camille and I waited for Daddy to dress and drive us to Fort Hamilton Army Base. The three of us tried to make small talk on the ride there. I was so nervous I didn't know what to do. Daddy dropped us off at the corner of their block.

"I'm going to be right up the street at that store on the corner. I ain't leaving you all here alone. So, when you get ready to head back, that's where I'll be," he said.

Holding hands, Camille and I walked up the walkway to her house.

Are you okay?" Camille asked before I rang the bell.

I nodded yes and pressed the bell. The door flung open and there she stood, just as I remembered her. She was smiling from ear to ear. She grabbed Camille and picked her up hugging her.

"Toni! Oh my baby!" she squealed.

"No, wait. I'm Camille. This is Toni!" Camille said. She put her down, embarrassed.

"I'm sorry. You two look like sisters," she said.

She hugged me tightly. Over her shoulder, I could see her two daughters. They were holding hands, both of them looking nervous.

"C'mon. Say hi to your sisters. This is Sherri. She's fourteen. This is Marie, she's ten. Go and say hi to your sister. Hug her!" she almost ordered them.

They walked to me and stood there. I said hello and we hugged awkwardly.

61

"Do you know that CJ died?" I had to ask. She acted like she would cry.

"Yes, baby. My mother called to tell me," she said.

"How did your mother know?" I asked curiously.

"Someone told her. I think it was one of your aunts. I was very hurt when I got the news," she said, leading us through the house into the kitchen.

I wasn't totally convinced that she was hurt since she didn't come to the funeral, nor did she try to contact us.

"Where were you?" I asked.

She took a platter of raw hamburger patties from the fridge. "I was in Texas then," she said.

She was right here in the United States and she couldn't come to her own baby's funeral! She offered Camille and me a seat in the back yard while she disappeared back into the kitchen. The girls stood in the doorway.

"Chill out, Toni," Camille whispered.

I could hear her saying something to the girls. She came outside with Paul, who looked the same to me except that he didn't have that ugly processed hairstyle anymore.

"Stand up and give me a hug," he said smiling.

I remembered how frightened I used to be when I heard that voice. Reluctantly I let him hug me. "She looks just like you, baby," he said to the woman that gave birth to me.

THROUGH THE FIRE

Camille, Sherri, Marie and I sat in the backyard under a large tree listening to the radio.

"Tell me some of the places you guys have lived," Camille asked.

"We've been to San Diego, Texas and Ohio and here," she said.

"What about Germany?" I asked.

"No, we haven't lived in Germany."

"Where were you born?" I asked, very curious now because when their mother left us, she and Paul were supposed to go to Germany for four years.

"I was born in San Diego. Marie was born in Texas," she replied.

"But didn't your father live in Germany?" I asked.

She was puzzled by my question, and it showed on her face.

"If he's been there, it was before I was born," she answered.

I sat chewing a smoked sausage while our mother clucked over Paul.

"Baby do you think you should put more salt on that potato salad? You know you have high blood pressure. Sherri, take that salt from your father," she said to Sherri.

She took the salt and handed it to Marie.

"Take this in the house, Marie," she said.

63

Marie got up and walked into the house. Paul was all smiles, watching her little ten-year-old behind walk away. I had a sick feeling in the pit of my stomach. Our eyes met, and he smiled and winked his eye at me. He made me sick to the stomach, yet I forced a smile. Marie came back to join us. She kept her eyes towards the ground, ashamed and frightened about something. Paul was molesting her like he used to do me. I could tell by the way he watched her, and the way she tried to avoid being seen.

"Would you like some peach cobbler and ice cream?" their mother asked me.

"I think I need to call my father so he can pick us up. It's getting late," I said.

None of my questions had been answered. I didn't know any more now, than I did before she showed back up in my life.

"We were going to take you home. Come on, stay," she said.

"Why did you leave me and CJ? What did we do to you?" I blurted.

Marie jumped up and ran inside the house.

Paul said, "Hold on now. She's still your mother!"

Sherri put her hands over her ears.

"I just want to know. You owe me that! I've not heard from you since I was five years old and suddenly you show up trying to act like nothing has happened. All of y'all sitting up here trying to act like thirteen years ain't passed. Y'all tryin' to act like I never lost my brother. In addition, like you didn't destroy our family. You've got to tell me why!"

Silence filled the back yard. It was so quiet that you could hear a rat piss on cotton.

"Go call your father and tell him it's time for you to leave," she said between clenched teeth.

"Damn it!" Paul said loudly standing up and knocking over the chair he was sitting in and stomping into the house.

I stood there staring at her with total hatred. She stared right back, just like she did when I was a child and she would push me away because I was hungry, or cold, or just wanted her to hug me. I hated her with so much of my being that I knew I couldn't wait for Daddy at her house.

"Don't you ever try to contact me again," I said quietly and left.

Camille and I walked up the block to the candy store on the corner. I saw Daddy's car sitting in front of it. He sat inside the store eating an Italian ice. I ran into his arms.

"I wasn't about to leave you alone with them fools. I didn't know what was going on and I was going to stay as close to you as possible. Let's go on home," he said putting his arm around me.

»Chapter 9«

I CALLED MICHAEL LATER ON that night and told him what had happened.

"I'm so sorry, Toni. I wish I could see you tonight," he said.

We made plans to meet the next day. We rode the train to the Village and walked around. Later, in a pizza parlor I told him all about it.

"I can't tell you what to do. However, you should give her a chance. My mother and father died when I was fifteen in a car accident. I wish I had a mother to get on my nerves," he said.

"I have a mother, okay. I don't need two. If she had wanted to be a mother, then she should have stayed with us instead of giving us away. Now she has to face the consequences," I said annoyed.

"Yeah, but Toni, maybe she can't answer those questions. If she were strung out on horse, then she was not herself. It's obvious she has changed if she has other children," he said.

"Oh yeah, she's changed alright. Paul is still the center of her universe, and she hasn't even noticed that he is messing with her daughters. Besides, I don't want to give her a chance. I don't ever want to see her sorry ass again as long as I live," I said.

Michael started to say something else, but I cut him off. "Let's not talk about her, okay?" I said.

"Okay," he said.

I was at Michael's house most of the day. Mommy thought I was at Camille's house. When Michael dropped me off on the corner that night around eight, I had no idea that the stuff had hit the fan. I walked inside the house to find no one at home. I didn't think too much of it, thinking that Mommy and Daddy had gone to dinner or a movie. I was just stepping out of the shower when I heard Mommy calling me. I wrapped a towel around me and went to her bedroom. She was packing some things of Daddy's into a suitcase.

"What's going on?" I asked.

"While you were out gallivanting around New York, your father fell down the basement stairs and broke his leg. I'm on my way to the hospital and when I come home, you need to be gone!" she said.

"What happened?" I asked worried about Daddy.

"Your father's in Jacobi Hospital because you were out with Michael when he needed you the most," she said tearfully.

"Let me get dressed so I can go with you," I said ignoring her comments because she was upset.

"No! You get your things and get out of my house!" she snapped angrily.

She was serious! I stomped back into my bedroom and slammed the door. If she wants me out, well then I'll leave. I can go stay with Michael, I thought. I threw some clothes into my suitcases and got my makeup from the bathroom. She got the nerve to want me to call her Mommy yet, the first time something goes wrong she reminds me that I'm not her child. How was I to know that my father would fall down the freaking stairs? Why wasn't she here? It could have happened if I had been home. She wants me out of her house? That was fine with me. I'll leave her house! Screw her! I fussed. I set my bags by the door and called Michael to come get me. I strutted to his car carrying my luggage and purse. I threw them into the back seat and slid in beside him.

"Where to?" he asked.

"Your place!" I said." Grinning from ear to ear, because I just knew that night I would be getting me some loving!

"Are you crazy? You're still in school. How are you going to take care of yourself?" he asked me.

"I can stay with you," I said. Yeah, I had it all figured out!

"You can't stay with me!" he said, acting as if he were surprised that I had even come up with that plan.

"Why not"? I asked shocked.

"Baby, you aren't even legal!" he said laughing.

"Michael!" I said angrily.

"Seriously, you need to go back home. Make peace with your folks. That's where you need to be. Toni, I can't let you stay with me because I love you and I want you to do the right thing," he said.

I stared at him in disbelief.

We looked through the newspaper and began to call people who had rooms to rent. I was so hurt and disappointed, but I just couldn't go back home if I wasn't wanted there.

Later, I went to the hospital to see Daddy. He was going to be fine. Unfortunately, there was a tension that existed between us and I didn't know why, nor did I ask him. After sitting there for many silent moments, I decided to leave. I kissed him on the cheek. He patted my hand and looked away quickly.

"Bye, Mommy" I said.

"Good bye," she replied. The way she said it, we both knew what she meant. "Don't be in my house when I get home!"

Michael had spoken to a Jamaican couple who had a rooming house on Broadway Street in Brooklyn. We walked to his car in silence to go and look at the room. It was cold and snowing that night. There was already seven inches of snow that had fallen in less than five hours. The wind blowing made the eighteen-degree weather feels like a minus twenty. A minus twenty degrees and I was homeless! I didn't know one doggone thing about Brooklyn, except Coney Island and Crown Heights. All of my trying to be the good daughter had failed. I felt so alone, I just wanted to disappear.

Michael talked to Mrs. Anderson while I stood sulking like the seventeen-year-old child that I was. He handed her the money for the room and kissed me good night. I watched as he walked to his car and drove away.

Mrs. Anderson gave me some clean sheets, a blanket and some towels and we went upstairs to the second floor. They owned a three-story brownstone. The second floor had three bedrooms, a kitchen, and a bathroom. On the third floor were three more bedrooms. She unlocked the door to the room that I would be renting. It was actually two rooms, a living room and a bedroom. Both were fixed up very nicely. She helped me to make the bed, talking a mile a minute the whole time. I was tired, cold and hungry. There were no places to eat around here, and I wasn't about to venture out of this house. It was so cold in my room that I could see my breath. After we made the bed, Mrs. Anderson showed me where the kitchen and bathroom were.

"Don't be leaving' your personals in de ba'room. You're not de only one to be using it. I have tr'ee males on dis floor, so keep your t'ings locked up and stay to yourself. Mr. Anderson and I will keep our ears out. You'll be safe. I ain't had no problems before. Don't 'spect to have none now. Just keep to yourself," she warned.

I nodded my head yes.

"You cold?" she asked me.

I must have nodded my head again. About thirty minutes after she left the room, she came back with two extra blankets, a portable heater, and Mr. Anderson carrying a big plate of food.

"I can tell you cold. We would keep de heat up higher, but the first two floors are like an oven. I give de tenants up here d'ese little heaters. Be careful with dem. I heard your stomach talking, so we got you some dinner. Clean de plate, now m' chile, and get some rest," she said, as she patted me on the shoulder, and then pulled me to her and hugged me.

I was definitely in need of a bath, but I wasn't about to take one that night. I put on my warmest pajamas, and plugged in the heater. The food was delicious and after I ate, I laid down to the best night of sleep I had in a long time. I got up at five the next morning to get ready for work. I didn't know how long it would take me to get to work from here, nor was I sure of the route. I tiptoed into the bathroom across the cold linoleum floor and splashed cold water on my face. I took a quick shower, cleaned the tub, as I had been told and hurried back into my bedroom. There were French doors on either side of my room. The glass had been painted with thick white paint, but I didn't know if there was a possibility that my neighbors could see me anyway, so I dressed in the near dark and put my makeup on after I got my clothes on. I made the bed and left for work. It was still dark outside when I stepped out on the slippery steps to walk the six blocks to the train station. I was very upset with my mother and tried to fight back the tears.

I wrapped my scarf tighter around my nose and mouth and started walking. The sidewalk was slick like ice, so I decided that it would be better if I walked in the middle of the street. The snow had melted so there was just slush in the street. When I finally got to the subway, my feet were frozen. There was no one in the station that morning, except me and the token booth clerk. I stood near his cage while I waited for the

71

subway. I cussed my parents all the way to work. I was nearly a half-hour early. I went to the cafeteria and ate breakfast. I tried to call my mother that day, but she refused to accept any calls from me. When I tried calling the hospital, my father told me that she had just left, or she had just gone down to the cafeteria, or some other lie.

"Daddy, please talk to her. I'm staying at this lousy rooming house. I have to stand outside and catch the train. How was I supposed to know that you were going to fall down the stairs?" I pleaded.

"I'll talk to her, but you know how Barbara is," he said.

When she finally returned my calls, she said that she was doing the best thing. "If you don't want to respect the rules of the house, well…you want to be an adult then you have to learn to make adult decisions and live with the consequences of those actions," blah blah blah...

I graduated that January and though my parents were there, they only said that they were proud of me. We went to Junior's restaurant in Brooklyn to celebrate together.

"Do you want us to drop you off at the train station or would you like to stay the night with us?" Mommy asked.

"I'd like to come home", I said. I got into the back seat of the Cadillac and rested my head against the window. Daddy had gotten a bottle of champagne and so we enjoyed a glass together and sat in the floor looking at old photo albums.

"You were so skinny when you came to live with Momma", Mommy said.

72

"If it wasn't for that mess of hair, she would disappear when she turned to the side," Daddy teased.

"You weren't a big man yourself. All of y'all looked like skeletons!" Mommy joked.

"Oh look, that's me on the first day of school. Aunt Liz took that picture. I looked so funny without teeth," I said. We laughed and talked until around midnight when we all began to get tired. I went up to my old room and lay down, thankful.

I was able to move back home that week. Spring would be coming up soon, and I certainly didn't want to be living in a houseful of hot, musty guys that I didn't know, and didn't like. I didn't want to have to walk pass all of those abandoned buildings that would be the hang out spot for every junkie and homeless person in Brooklyn. I was so glad to be home. I had begun to work full time at the Post just for the summer. In August, I started attending Medgar Evers College. I wanted to one day own my own business, so I planned to major in Business after my first year. Right now, I was studying journalism. Michael and I didn't have that much time to spend together. His oldest son was visiting him for the summer, so I only was able to see him a couple of times during the week.

One Sunday I decided to surprise him with a visit. When I got to his apartment, Tina was there preparing dinner for them. She moved around in the kitchen like she lived there. I followed Michael back to his room, and shut the door behind me. "What is she doing here?" I asked.

"She's fixing dinner for me and the boys," he said.

73

"If you all were hungry, and I am supposed to be your woman, why didn't you call me to come over and fix dinner for you"? I asked.

"Toni, Tina and her mother are having some problems and she's been staying here for about two weeks. As soon as she gets an apartment of her own, she's moving," he said.

"You know what, I'm about sick of this," I said. I grabbed my purse and walked out. I fussed to myself all the way back to Queens.

I decided that I was not going to call him or try to contact him. My family was planning to purchase four brownstones on Lafayette Street in Brooklyn and was just waiting for the closing date to be set. Since, Michael wasn't trying to contact me, and I wasn't trying to contact him, he didn't know we were about to move. We had been in the new house about three weeks before I decided to call him and give him my new phone number. Boy was he upset! "Well the phone system works both ways. I don't remember you trying to call me either," I snapped.

"You told me not to call you at your parent's house," he snapped back.

We both started laughing at how silly we sounded. We made plans to meet later on during the week because he said he had something important to talk to me about.

That day he told me that he had plans to join the military. He said that he wanted to be a dentist, and that as long as he worked he would never be able to attend school. He said that he would be twenty-five in seven months and he needed to join before then, otherwise he would never do it. I was going to stand behind him no matter what plans he decided to undertake. In March of 1976, he joined the Air Force and was sent to San Antonio, Texas for his basic training. It was not possible to call him that often while he was in basic training, so we wrote each other. I longed to receive his letters. They were always so short. I wanted to know more about what was going on with him, but he told me that he was not a writer. My letters were ten and twelve pages. After his six-week basic training was over, he had two days free before he would be attending Technical school, so I flew down to Texas to see him. At the airport, he suggested very excitedly that we should get married. It was a Friday evening, way after five. We had not had a blood test done yet, nor did we have a marriage license, but I agreed that we should do it.

We got a hotel room and I pulled out the telephone directory and began calling around trying to find out how to get a marriage license in this town. I found out that the Clerk of Court's office is where you get a license. The Clerk's name was Rosetta Phelps. I looked through the residence directory and found her home phone number. I called her and explained our situation. She was very apprehensive at first, but finally agreed to meet us at the courthouse. She told me that I might want to go to the Health Department and see if they would do a blood test.

They held an evening clinic for diabetes patients. I called them and explained that I was just visiting for a couple of days, and we hadn't had a chance to get a blood test, and I begged like a dog until the nurse agreed to give us a blood test. Michael borrowed one of his friend's cars and we went first to the clinic and then to the Courthouse. We got the license and were on our way out when Mrs. Phelps suggested that we just go down to the sixth floor where the judge was performing numerous weddings. When we arrived there, both of us in jeans and t-shirts, we signed the register and waited until our names were called. That is how we were wed.

After the ceremony, we stood outside on the steps and kissed for a very long time. I had never loved anyone like I loved him and I swore to him that I would do everything in my power to make him happy. He promised that he would never hurt me, and would always be there for me. I looked into those big brown eyes and believed with all of my heart that he meant every word of it.

»Chapter 10«

BACK AT THE HOTEL, HE wanted to make love to me right away. I wanted to make this as romantic as possible; considering that, we had waited so long for this moment. We went to dinner down by the Riverside Walkway and then we went for a stroll before going back to the hotel. We stopped every few feet and kissed passionately.

"I promise you, that I will never hurt you. I love you, girl," he said. We showered together and I put on a black teddy that I had packed just in case.

I had read so many romance novels that I was very disillusioned about sex. Making love with him was not at all, like I had read about. After kissing me and touching my breasts, he just seemed to be in a hurry. I squirmed beneath him, trying to get comfortable. He stopped for a few minutes, holding me and trying to soothe me.

"Just relax. It will only hurt for a minute," he said.

Five minutes later, he was finished. I just didn't expect that it would be so quick. Michael kept thanking me repeatedly, so I must have done something right. Still I felt that something was missing. After about thirty minutes, we made love again. In fact, we made love several times before daybreak. Each time was the same as the other. I wanted him to kiss me there, like he had kissed me back in Brooklyn at Danny's party. I didn't know how to suggest it, and he didn't make any moves towards that direction. We fell asleep in each other's arms just as the sun was coming up. The next day we never left the room. On Sunday morning, I was on a plane heading back to New York. It was our plans for me to join him after Technical school, which was an eight-week course. He was training to be a police officer.

My parents were upset, but there was nothing that they could do now.

"I want you to promise me that you will finish college and get your degree. You've always said that you want to get your master's degree. If I can find time to go to school, so can you," Daddy said.

"What? You didn't tell me that you are going to school," I said. I was so proud of him.

"Yeah, I want to own my own business too. I've been thinking about buying a restaurant. There's one available for sale right around the corner from here. I know what you're getting ready to say. That's what I'm going to school for, to be a chef," he said. I was remembering the days of his burnt bologna and egg sandwiches.

"I'll finish school, Daddy, I promise you that," I said.

Camille took me out to dinner. "Well, we knew it was going to happen one day, right?" she said fighting back the tears.

"Girl, I'm going to miss you," I cried in her arms.

78

"You're going to be just fine. You better get back in school real quick, otherwise you never will," she said.

I promised Camille that when I joined Michael wherever he would be sent, I would stay in touch with her. Unfortunately, we lost touch before I even left New York. Camille married a man from Nigeria and moved to his country.

Michael and I were able to talk every day while he was in Tech school. I missed him so much, and couldn't wait to see him. Then he got his orders, and we would be spending the next four years in New Mexico. I had never been there, and was quite excited to be seeing another part of the country. We brought an olive green Vega and headed west. I think Michael had about fifty dollars with him, until we got to New Mexico. I had about four hundred dollars with me. One hundred miles from San Antonio, the car broke down. It was two miles to the nearest gas station and we walked every step of it. After getting the mechanic, we rode back in a beat up, greasy pick-up to where the car was to see if he could fix it. He told us that we had a busted head gasket and that the radiator hose was leaking. He would not be able to get to it until the next day. We had to stay in a hotel. The cheapest hotel there was the Motel 6 and it was filthy. We were newlyweds and we were just glad the room had a bed. We showered that night and sat on the bed eating a bucket of Kentucky Fried Chicken and drinking some Thunderbird and ginger ale!

It cost nearly four hundred dollars to get the car fixed! The mechanic didn't complete the car until nearly six that evening. We drove until we got tired and then we pulled into a rest stop. We were down to seven dollars, not enough to get us to New

Mexico. Michael called Brian in New York, and he wired us a hundred dollars. We filled the tank with gas and started again, and then the muffler fell off the car. We heard it when it hit the road and was run over by a diesel truck. We just laughed it off and kept driving. By now, the car was sounding like a small two engine plane. We were so in love that we didn't care that people passed our car, pointing and laughing at us. We were in love!

It was five o'clock in the evening when we drove into Alamogordo, New Mexico. Neither of us had seen anything like this. There were tumbleweeds that blew across the road, just like on the westerns. I saw a roadrunner that looked just like the one in the cartoon, and on every corner was a car lot, and a Mexican restaurant. The base was about ten miles from the town. There was desert all around. We drove silently to our destination, the last ten miles. Michael was looking out of his side of the window and I was looking out mine.

"Look, a coyote!" I said excitedly.

"Look, a buffalo," he said.

"An Indian," I said.

"How do you know that?" he asked.

"His tags said COCHISE," I replied.

When we got to Holloman Air Force Base, we were asked to pull over and another officer came to the car. The guards wore navy blue dress slacks and light blue shirts with white ascots. Their black leather boots were laced with white laces and you could see your face in the shine. They examined Michael's documents and told us where we could find "lodging". I knew that we were definitely on a military base then. We drove until we saw a sign that said "Billeting". This was the place where we could get a room with an adjoining bath. Our neighbors the first night were a white airman and his oriental wife. I would see many interracial couples during our stay here.

After getting our luggage out of the car, we decided that we better count our money and see where there was to eat for cheap. I checked my wallet and to my amazement, I had twelve cents! Michael had one dollar and a few pennies. We laughed.

"I got an idea. When we were driving through town, I saw a Chinese restaurant. We'll go there, explain to the owners that we just got here and won't have any money until the bank opens tomorrow when you can cash your check and see if she will let us eat and pay her tomorrow," I said.

"Are you crazy? Ain't nobody gonna let us eat and pay them the next day," he said.

"Let's just try it," I said. We showered and were changed. We rode back downtown and found the restaurant. He was afraid to be seen with me when I asked, just in case I got the "No" answer. He waited in the front of the building and I walked around to the drive-thru window. There was a Chinese woman standing there. I explained to her our situation and she welcomed us in. I went around to the front to get Michael and together we went inside. Three waiters were getting a room ready towards the back of the restaurant. We went in and they shut the divider. From the kitchen, they began bringing plates and plates full of food; fried rice, egg foo young, chicken dishes, sweet and sour shrimp, egg rolls. There was enough food there to feed ten people. It was very nice. The next day when we returned to pay her, she refused to accept the money. We ate there regularly after that of, but of course, we had to pay for our meals.

After Michael cashed his check, he opened an account at the credit union, which he was advised to do in the information packet that was given us before we left San Antonio. It also suggested signing up for base housing. We moved into a mobile home park about five miles from the base. All of the homes looked exactly alike, beige with brown shutters. There must have been a hundred of them. They were lined up in neat rows going on for what looked like a half mile, with rows of at least twenty homes. They were all furnished with the same ugly furniture. We had two days before Michael had to report to work. We looked around the town, finding places of interest and what not. We met some of our neighbors as well. This was going to be very different for the both of us, but we looked forward to it together.

The closets in our bedroom were not big enough to hold all of our clothes, so Michael put his things in the spare room. He started acting very strange when I picked up his little green suitcase. "No, I'm just going to put that under the bed. I'm not going to unpack it," he said quickly taking it from me and sliding it under the bed. It was out of sight, but not out of mind. That evening the little green suitcase seemed to be calling me. I went to the spare room and sat down on the bed after he had fallen asleep. I peeked under the bed, but it was not there anymore. I got down on the floor and looked again, but it was gone for sure. I wasn't even surprised. I opened the closet door and it was hid under some sweaters. He had also put green electrical tape over the taps. That really made me more suspicious. I put things back like there were and went back to bed.

The next morning, after Michael went to work, I began to unpack the rest of our things. That's when I remembered the little green suitcase. I went to the spare room and took the suitcase down from the shelf. I sat down on the bed and carefully removed the tape and put them on the edge of the dresser. I opened the suitcase and there were over a hundred letters in there. They were organized in bunches held together with rubber bands. Every single one of them was from Tina. She had written him every day that he was in basic training and technical school. In fact, some of them had the same postmark, where she had mailed off two or three letters in one day! I glanced out of the window to make sure that Michael hadn't come back, and I began to read the letters. I read a few, and put them back in the bunch. Michael had led Tina to believe that he would marry her and she would be joining him in New Mexico. She had enrolled in a program and gotten her GED.

She wanted him to look around for her a job, and send her some applications. She ended all of the letters that I had time to read with from you future wife. I put the tape back over the tabs, and put the suitcase back on the shelf. Even though I was very upset, I didn't say anything to him about it that first day. I could hardly wait for him to leave in the mornings so that I could begin to read these letters. It must have taken me a week to read the entire suitcase of letters. She had even sent him pictures. That Easter she had volunteered to play the Easter bunny at her son's school. She had a picture of herself with

83

this big pink rabbit outfit on, and then there was a picture where she just had on a pink teddy and the bunny ears. It was taken with a Polaroid camera. At the bottom of the picture, she had written, *just for you, Daddy*. Well by the end of the week, I was livid.

»Chapter 11«

WHEN MICHAEL CAME HOME that night, I was so mad that I could have killed a puppy. I wasn't sure if I should tell him that I had read the letters from Tina, after all I had invaded his privacy. However, he should have not saved the letters, especially when he knew that he was going to be getting married to another woman. No, he should have thrown them out. Yet, I should have respected him enough to leave his things alone. It went on like that all evening, me battling with myself about the letters.

"What's wrong, you're awfully quiet?" he kept saying to me. I would comment that all was well, but I was seething inside.

Finally, after we had gotten in the bed, I told him that I had read his letters from Tina. He looked a little surprised, but he didn't try to lie his way out of it or feed me some bull about them. I wanted to know why he had led her to believe that she would be coming with him to New Mexico. One of the letters he had gotten from her was just a couple of days after we had gotten married.

"Well, I told her that I was going to marry you, and she said that she would sue me for child support if I did. I figured that I would hold her off until after the wedding and then tell her. You see, I have been giving her money all of these years for Remy, but not through the courts. I never thought to save any receipts or anything, so if we went to court she could say I never gave her anything. I wanted to wait until after the wedding and then explain to her," he said.

"Have you explained it to her?" I asked.

"Not yet, but I will," he said. I let it go that night.

A few days later, he was watching the game and I was lying across the bed watching a movie on the other television set when the phone rang. It was Tina calling collect to speak to Michael. I accepted the charges. "Let me speak to Michael," she snapped without saying hello to me.

"Hello Tina and how are you?" I asked.

"Let me speak to Michael," she repeated.

He picked up the other line and they must have talked and laughed for nearly an hour. When he was finished, I asked him if Remy was fine. "I guess so," he said.

"What do you mean you guess so? You didn't talk to him?" I asked.

"No, he wasn't home," he said.

"So what were you two talking about?" I asked.

"Just stuff that's happening in the neighborhood," he said.

Each Sunday she called to talk to him about "stuff happening in the neighborhood."

I finally decided to let him know that I didn't like it. I could understand it if she were letting him talk to his son, but most of the time he wasn't even home. They just talked about things going on in the neighborhood, and old friends that they shared. I was jealous and didn't want her calling like that every Sunday. He couldn't understand why I would get upset.

"Michael, the entire time we were dating, this woman was in and out of your house. You constantly used the excuse that it was because she was your son's mother, but that is bull, okay. Now, I let it go back then, but I am not going to put up with it now. On top of that, we can't afford to keep paying these high phone bills. I want to get back into school, and you said that you do too. So, you tell her to stop calling every Sunday, or I will," I said, trying to sound calm when I really just wanted to scream at him from the top of my lungs.

Michael and I went to the base together to file for base housing. A female soldier took our application. Her nametag read Captain Cynthia Box. She had a very thick West Indian accent. She called our names three times before we understood what she was even saying. After we sat down, she began to ask Michael many questions, but was not doing that much writing on our application. She must have thought I was stupid, because she was openly flirting with my husband with me sitting right there.

However, I didn't get too upset about it because she appeared to be at least twenty years older than we were. She was asking him questions that I thought had to be military lingo, for example, she asked him what his MOS was and if he planned to stay in for life. She even asked some that I thought was quite personal.

"Are you two planning on having children? How long have you two been married?" She turned to me and asked, "Do you work?"

When we got outside, I teased Michael. "That old lady likes you!"

"You must be crazy. She ain't my type!" he said picking me up and carrying me to the car laughing like two fools. I looked back at the office and saw that Captain Box was standing in the doorway watching.

Barbie and her husband Wes were from Hollis, New York. They had a two-month-old son named Jamal. They also lived in one of the trailers four doors down from us. They had been in New Mexico over a year. She was very familiar with the area. Wes would leave Barbie the car and she would drive me around to all the places of interest. Barbie and I became very close friends.

Though I had friends, I missed Mommy. I wrote her about two or three times a month, because I could only afford to call her once a month, but she called me every Sunday. We would talk for at least an hour before she handed the phone to Daddy. After he had asked the four basic questions that fathers ask their daughters -is he treating you right, do you need any money, when are you coming to see us, are you in school, he would say good-bye.

THROUGH THE FIRE

I enrolled in college that fall full time. To fill my evenings, Barbie and I had enrolled in a ceramics class and an aerobics class. We took up needlepoint, tie dying and dance classes. We were busy nearly every waking hour. Michael worked five days and was off seven. Then he would work seven days and be off five. Barbie's husband had more of a normal schedule. He worked five days a week, from eight am to five pm. Therefore, she had to bow out of many of the things that we had gotten involved in so she could spend time with him. As a result, I had to meet someone else that could hang with me on those days.

I met Vanessa, whom everyone called by her nickname Tootie. She was biracial, tall, slender and beautiful, with waist length, light brown curly hair. Her husband worked sporadic shifts like Michael, so, it was a while before I was able to meet him, and I was shocked to say the least. Tootie had not said much about her husband and so I didn't know what to expect, but looking at her and her two handsome sons, I just assumed that he was a good-looking man. He was what folks called U-ga-lie!

I had never in my entire life seen anyone that unattractive before, nor since, and he had the nerve to be rude. While she was introducing me to him, he just walked away. Tootie was embarrassed and apologized for him. I knew that it was best if I leave, so we made plans to get together the next day.

When I introduced Tootie to Barbie, she could not stand Tootie and made it obvious that she didn't like her. When I introduced my husband to Tootie, he said that there was something about her that he didn't like.

"What is it?" I asked him.

89

"I think it is her hair. It's so wild," he remarked.

"Her hair? Is that the best you can come up with? My hair would be wild too, if it wasn't for Dippity Do!" I reminded him. My hair was to my shoulders and most of the time I just wore it in a ponytail because it had a mind of its own. I didn't want to perm it, because it was half way straight naturally, but when I did wear it out, it was wild! He had told me many times that I looked like a lion, yet he didn't want me to cut it.

The military lifestyle was different from anything that I had ever encountered. All of us were hundreds of miles from family and friends. There was a small clique of black folks at Holloman and every one of us knew each other. If we didn't know the name, we knew the face and where they lived. However, I did get some real tight sister friends. Through Barbie, I met Denise, whom we called Necy. I met Liz through Necy. I met Sharon though Liz. All four of them were married and had kids. When their husbands took them out, I usually had a house full of babies running around wild.

On some Friday nights, we would get together at my house and I would fry fish and potatoes and make a salad. Michael would get several six packs and we would have card parties, or play Scrabble in teams of two. No one wanted to have Michael on their team because he always took the longest to put down a word. We would make a pallet in the floor in the spare room and have babies all over the place, and the bigger kids on the bed. It would sometimes be six in the morning before we would finish playing. Everyone that I introduced Tootie to felt that she was bad news and warned me about her. Since I didn't see any of the things that they saw, I continued to hang with her.

Late nights, when both of our husbands were at work, and her boys had been put down for the night, I would go over to her house. She lived just across the dirt path from me. She wasn't a good housekeeper and to top that off, she had a puppy. Her house always smelled of diaper buckets, wet puppy, and fried food. I liked her because she was a very interesting person. She was very intelligent, but the desire to continue her education was downplayed by her dominating husband. She had the potential and desire to do many things, but he made fun of her ideas and dreams. She stopped telling him about them, and began to confide in me. We would make popcorn, get a six-pack, a nickel bag and talk about life, people and things in general. Around five or six in the morning, I would go back home to my own little tin cabin. That's what we called little two bedroom mobile homes that we lived in. Even though it was furnished, and all of them had the same plain furniture, I had tried to personalize our home. I brought curtains and hung them at all of the windows. I got some beautiful plants and trees, and some nice pictures. It didn't matter it still looked like a tin cabin.

»Chapter 12«

WHEN MY HUSBAND CAME HOME and wanted to know what I had done all night, I would tell him part of it. I went to Tootie's, where we talked, had a couple of beers and watched television. He was a police officer and I didn't dare let him know that I had smoked weed nearly all night. I fixed him a light breakfast every morning when he got home and we would fool around a while before he dozed off into a deep sleep that took him far into the day. While he was sleeping, I would go to school downtown. My last class was over at 2:30 in the afternoon. At three, I would go to my ceramics class. I would have dinner with Barbie or Necy, and then go to our African dance class. They would usually go to another of our friends' house and play whiz or a board game for pennies. I wasn't interested in that, so I usually hooked up with Tootie. She and I would take her boys to the only zoo in town and then the park. While they played, we shared a joint and talked about life.

Tootie had something to tell me. I knew that by the way she always brought up the subject on interracial relationships. I knew that she was light complexion, and all of us had assumed that because of that, her gray eyes, and long Chaka Khan wild hair that she was definitely mixed. I had never asked, but I knew that she was going to tell me something concerning that. I respected her enough to wait and let her tell me when she was ready, so one night, after the boys were in bed; I went to her house as usual. I was shocked when she opened the door, because the smell of Lysol hit me. Her house was spotless. She had put up some beige curtains in the living room and had some dried flowers sitting in the middle of the dining table.

"Girl, what have you done?" I asked.

"I just thought I would clean up. I got sick of this place. I told Ricky to take that puppy back to the pound. I was sick of him messing up my carpet and the boys' bed with do-do and stuff," she said. She was smiling, glad that I had noticed and approved. I hugged her. I didn't have that kind of relationship with Barbie or Necy.

"I got a check from my Mom today, so I got us some champale!" she said strutting over to the refrigerator. She had it chilling in the freezer.

"Go 'head!" I joked.

Deep into our conversation, she asked me how I met Michael. "When I was sixteen years old, I was at Coney Island one Saturday. I was on a ride, and he was standing there watching me. Girl, I thought he was the finest man on earth. He took me for a Coke - a Coca-Cola that is," I laughed. "My parents didn't want us together. They hated Michael. They even threw me out of the house because I wouldn't stop seeing him. I was still in school, so you know I was mad with them," I said. We laughed, but I really didn't think it was funny, I married him anyway and the rest is history. "What about you and Ricky?" I asked.

93

She took a long drag of the joint and a big gulp of champale. "I knew him in high school. I was very popular in school. With the boys, that is. The girls couldn't stand me. They said I thought I was better than them, but that wasn't true because I came from the worst projects in East St. Louis. Anyway, when I was in the tenth grade year Ricky just walked up to me one day and asked me to go with him to the prom. I didn't even know who he was. When I looked past him, I saw all of these guys watching, waiting, like they had made a bet or something with him, so I told him that I would go with him. I had on an ugly hot pink gown that my Mommy got at a five and dime store, girl. She had a lady friend of hers press my hair. I had these great big Shirley temple curls or whatever you called them and the hair was piled up this high on my head. I looked like Dolly Parton, except, I ain't got no boobs. We didn't even dance. All he wanted to do was sit and hold my hand and stare at me all night. We had to ride the bus one top of that. After the prom, he had to take me home. My Mom was very strict, right, so at my door he asked *'So, can I kiss you good night?'* I knew too that kissing me was probably part of the bet, so I let him kiss me. He couldn't kiss, girl. He just jammed his tongue in my mouth and spit all over my face. I was so disgusted.

After that, he was always coming around my way. Eventually, I got pregnant with Little Ricky and my Mom threw me out of the house. I had no choice but to marry him. He didn't have no job, or nothing. We had to live with his Mom and three sisters and brothers. We shared a room with his little brother. His brother had bunk beds! Girl, I hated it. I hated him for putting me there. He got his GED and joined the Air Force. I stayed with his Mom until he sent for me when he got here, and right after I got here, I got pregnant with Jerome. I wanted to have my tubes tied after him, but he said he wants six sons. That nigga is crazy if he thinks that I am going to have another kid. After we got here, we started having money problems. He was mad about something. I don't know. We're only nineteen. It's too much responsibility for both of us. I can say that and not be ashamed, but he doesn't see it like I do. He is always talking about 'I'm the man in the house. What I say goes', but I think married people are supposed to be a team. He doesn't ever want to talk to me. He doesn't care what me and the boys do during the day. He's just in his own little world. Then one day girl, out the clear blue sky he hit me. He hit me so hard I saw stars. I fell to the floor and he was on me, just hitting me and hitting me. I called his CO," she said.

"Did he cut you?" I asked referring to the scar that went from her left ear all the way to the corner of her mouth.

She had another scar on her throat from one ear to the other ear, like a razor blade had cut her. I hoped that she had been in a car accident or something. I didn't want to hear that something violent had happened to her.

"When I was fourteen years old, I met this dude. His name was Lonnie Williams III. He was a drug pusher and bookie. He thought he was fine, girl. Every woman wanted him. He had this old woman named Clara Barnes. She was mean and ugly. If she heard that someone had even looked at Lonnie she would cut them up. She wouldn't kill them, just disfigure them. My uncle owned a small candy store and he had this old man run his numbers for him, but he kept being arrested, so, my uncle asked my Mom if I could be his runner. He said that no one

95

would suspect a kid, right. He offered my Mom a cut of his profits and she said yes, so, I started running his numbers for him. I had to go to Lonnie Williams and pick up this brown paper bag every day. One day I went over there. There was no one there but him. He raped me. The word got back to Clara and she was waiting for me in front of the school one day. She didn't even say anything. I saw her sitting on the side of a car with her legs crossed waiting, but I didn't think she was waiting on me, right. Someone must have seen me at their house longer than usual, because they told her that I had been going over there sleeping with Lonnie Williams. She slid off the car and walked up to me. "You Tootie?" she asked. I nodded my head yes and all I saw was her hand go up and that's all. She cut my face first. I was with my baby brother. He helped me to the wall of the school and sat me down. Told me not to move around because the more I moved the more it bled. I was leaning against the wall, my head down and she came over and sat down beside me. The bitch yanked my hair, pulled my head back, and cut my throat from ear to ear. I knew I was going to be dead by the time my brother got back. I just sat there. Blood was all over the front of my clothes and running down into my lap like a waterfall. An ambulance came and took me to the hospital."

"My mom is just as mean as Clara Barnes. That night she and my uncle who owned the candy store went riding. That's what they call it in St. Louis. They found Lonnie Williams III first. He was collecting money from his whores downtown. My uncle walked up to him and pumped five bullets into his head, and they got back into the car and went looking for Clara Barnes. My Mom had my uncle hold her. She reached into

Clara's bra and took out the razor blade. She cut her just like she cut me. 'Cept she cut her throat so she would die. They never even went to jail. They have this Victim's Assistance Program in my state for victims of violent crimes. When I turn twenty-one I'm supposed to get some money for it, a settlement," she said. I hugged her and we sat there crying. I felt so bad for her."

I never told anyone what happened to Tootie; not even Michael. She confided in me, and I wasn't going to betray her trust. I loved her like she was my sister. We spent a lot of time together until she got housing on the base. I had no way of seeing her every day now because my husband needed the car, and I didn't know how to drive. I begged Michael to give me driving lessons. I studied the manual and went down town to get my license. It took me three times of trying to finally get them. By this time, we had been called to get base housing and I was pregnant with our first child.

One morning, during my fourth month, I woke with these excruciating cramps. I called my doctor and he sent an ambulance for me. I called Michael and he said that he would meet me at the hospital. I was bleeding now and knew that I was going to lose the baby. I could tell from the sullen faces of the paramedics as they worked quickly trying to help me. I started crying and couldn't calm down. At four o'clock that evening, I lost our baby. I was kept overnight for tests and released the next day. I was devastated. I stayed in the bed all of the next three or four days. Michael took those days off from work and stayed with me. "It's okay, baby. We'll try again," he assured me. When he returned to work, Tootie came by. I didn't even have to talk with her. I just laid my head in her lap and cried. She stroked my hair and sang softly. I fell asleep for the first time in three days without medication. When I woke up, Tootie had prepared my dinner and straightened up my house. She left a note on the refrigerator to call her if I needed her.

It took a while to get over losing my child. I lay awake at night thinking about babies. My Mom offered to come out and I let her. I hadn't seen her in so long. There comes an experience in one's life where no matter how many friends you have with you, nothing can soothe you like your mother. I didn't even have the energy to ride the twenty miles to the airport with Michael to pick her up. I did take a shower and fix my face so that I would look half way decent when they arrived. I sat on the porch waiting for them. When I saw the car turning the corner, I stood on the curb crying. My mother never looked so good, her arms never felt so good.

For the next three weeks, she nursed me both physically and mentally. I had really missed her. She and Michael surprised me one day with a beautiful black Ford Mustang as a gift. I hated it when she had to return to New York. We stood hugging good-bye and crying until the third announcement was made about her flight boarding. Michael was so sympathetic to my needs during this time. When we returned to the base, we cuddled up in front of the television, watched old movies, and ate huge bowls of ice cream. That night he wanted to make love to me, but I wasn't ready. I felt like such a failure for losing the baby. In my mind, I felt that I wasn't ready to get pregnant again, for fear of losing another baby. I equated having sex with getting pregnant. He said he understood.

However, the next day he turned to me again, and I had to refuse. On the fourth refusal, he became angry.

"Why can't I make love to you?" he demanded. I tried to explain it to him. "I didn't say 'let's make a baby'. I said let's make love. There is a difference," he said.

"I'm just not ready yet," I said. He went into the bathroom and slammed the door loudly. In a few minutes, he went into our bedroom and shut the door. When he came out, he was dressed in casual clothes, and smelling of cologne.

"I'll be home in a few hours," he said on his way out the door. I cried a while and called Tootie to come over. She knew exactly what I was trying to say.

"He'll be all right. Just give him time. Men don't understand about miscarriages. To us, a baby died. To them it ain't a baby until it's born," she said trying to reassure me. She was right. He didn't see it as our losing our child. I needed time to mourn.

When he got home that night, it was well after three in the morning. He slipped quietly into the bed beside me. I turned towards him and put my arm around him.

"I'm sorry about earlier. Please forgive me," I whispered against his neck. He turned to me and kissed me tenderly.

"I'm the one that should be sorry," he said. We held each other all night and talked.

A few days later, I was cleaning the oven when the phone rang.

"May I speak to Michael," said the voice on the other end.

She had a very heavy West Indian accent. I assumed that it was someone that he worked with. His female co-workers had called our home before to ask him to switch shifts with them, or to see about getting a ride, so I didn't think anything of this call. I told the woman that Michael wasn't in yet and asked if she wanted to leave a message. She hung up abruptly.

It had been two months since the miscarriage and still I could not bring myself to make love with Michael. We would pet and touch, but I just would freak out when he wanted to do more. He would storm out of the bed and sit in the living room watching Saturday Night Live reruns. I wanted him to understand and be patient with me.

I came home from the supermarket one Saturday morning and overheard Michael discussing our problems with Tina on the phone. When he got off, I told him that our business was between us, and I didn't appreciate him discussing us with her.

"She's my son's mother, I can talk to her about whatever I want to!" he snapped and walked out of the kitchen. I went right behind him.

"What is that supposed to mean?" I asked hurt.

"It means just what I said!" he said.

We stood there staring at each other angrily. That remarked implied that at least she could have my child. I got my purse and went for a ride in my new car, my hair blowing in the wind. I parked on the hill overlooking the college and smoked a joint.

Later that week I received another call from the West Indian woman. Again, I asked her if she wanted to leave Michael a message, and she hung up. This time I asked him about her. He said that he didn't know who it could be.

A couple days later, she called again. This time it was nearly two in the morning. She woke me up from a very deep, drug-induced sleep.

"No, Michael isn't home," I said.

"I know that, he just left my house. He's a wonderful lover. Why won't you make love with him?" she asked and then hung up the phone.

I knew I had to be dreaming, but I was sitting here holding the phone in my hands at two in the morning, and his side of the bed was empty. He had told me that one of his co- workers was going to Greece and that his company was giving him a going away party. I trusted him because I didn't have any reason not to, not until now. I lay awake until he came home about thirty minutes later. I told him immediately about the call. He laughed and told me that someone was messing with my head, but I didn't see anything funny about it. He didn't want to talk about it, and made it very clear when he got into the bed and pulled the covers over his ears. I turned my back to him, seething all that night.

I called Tootie and told her about it as soon as I knew that her husband was asleep that morning.

"Didn't you tell me that he told you one time that he had to have sex, back when you were first seeing him?" she asked.

101

I had nearly forgotten that he had told me that. He wouldn't cheat on me, would he? When he got up that morning, I fixed his breakfast, just like always. While he was eating his pancakes, I asked him directly if he was seeing someone.

"No, I am not seeing anyone, and I resent the fact that you would even ask me something like that. You know how I feel about you," he said, acting annoyed.

I reminded him that he told me when we first started seeing each other that he had to have sex.

"I was young then," he snapped and walked away.

I let it go, but he was beginning to act strangely. He would go out every night that he was not working. I wanted to go with him just like before the miscarriage, but he blew me off with any kind of vague excuse. I hoped that he would come around soon.

»CHAPTER 13«

ONE OCTOBER NIGHT, MICHAEL called me about ten minutes before ten. I was trying to catch the last few minutes of the Jefferson's. Billy Dee Williams was a guest on the show that night. He was Florence the house cleaner's idol, and she was really tripping. Michael's car was in the shop, and I was supposed to pick him up from work.

"Toni, there's been a shooting. Don't come down here tonight. I want you to go over to Wes' house. I'll call you when I can get home," he said quickly, before hanging up the phone.

I called Barbie, who had seen it on the news. I told her that I was on my way to her house, to be looking out for me. She lived just a block from me. I got my sneakers, turned off all the lights, locked the doors and ran to her house. She was waiting for me on the porch. All of the lights were off in her house. She said that the news reported that a military policeman had gone berserk and shot, killed several people, and then ran off in the direction of the housing area with his weapon and several rounds of ammunition. We went inside and Wes locked everything up, and closed the blinds. We all went up to the second floor and waited in the dark. The night was very quiet except for the bullfrogs and Jamal. The sky was a beautiful orange, navy blue and lit up by the full moon.

"All kinds of weird things happen on the full moon," Wes said.
103

"Baby, doesn't anybody want to hear the full moon stories'"
Barbie said laughing.

"I want to hear about them," I said.

He had lived in the Breevort Projects, which was a housing
project in the Bedford/Stuyvesant section of Brooklyn. His
parents were from Mississippi. We had all kinds of jokes about
people from Mississippi that had migrated to the north. Barbie
was originally from Jamaica.

"Let him tell his story, Barbie," I said defending him.

We sat on the floor in the dark, listening to Wes tell us all
kinds of stupid stories of things that had happened on the full
moon. I was laughing, but I was worried about my husband
being out there looking for this fool who had enough
ammunition to kill every police officer on duty.

Around three that morning we heard on the news that the killer
had been caught. A couple hours later Michael came to pick me
up. The front of his shirt and pants were covered in blood.

"He died right there in my arms. It was terrible. I have never
seen anything like it before. And don't want to see nothing like
it again," he whispered, as I held him that morning.

I stroked his head and kissed his tears away. I loved him so
much, and felt so badly for him. I took his uniform, wrapped it
in newspaper and threw it in the dumpster in the alley behind
our house. It was eight o'clock in the morning, and the flag
that was on the corner of my street at the Officer's Club was
flying half-staff. I went back inside just as Michael was
hanging up the phone.

"Who was that?" I asked.

It appeared that he was talking and then saw me, and hung up without giving the person on the other end a warning. "Wrong number," he mumbled. However, I didn't even hear the phone ring unless it rang while I was in the alley for those three seconds.

I showered and went back to bed, and no sooner than I had gotten in the bed, he got up.

"I need to go down to the station. We all have to write a report of what happened," he said, avoiding making eye contact with me.

"Are you okay?" I asked. He looked at me then.

"Yeah, I'm just a little shaken up," he said.

"Do you want me to go with you? Drive you?" I asked.

"No, Darryl is going to pick me up," he said. He walked past me and went into the kitchen.

"Do you have time for breakfast?" I asked.

"I'll just get a bagel," he said, taking it with him and walking outside.

A police car picked him up and he was gone. I cleaned up the house and tried to catch the story on the news. When he came back a couple of hours later, I asked him what had happened to cause this man to snap.

"It's a police matter, and I can't discuss it with you," he said.

DARBY WEST

I thought he was kidding with me. I asked him about it again later on that day.

"Toni, didn't I say I can't discuss it? Let it go, okay," he replied.

I was beginning to think my husband was crazy. He would be so sweet one minute and then the phone would ring, and he would be whispering to someone for a few seconds and would hang up.

"Who was that?" I would ask.

"Do I ask you who you are talking to every time the phone rings? Dang!" he would snap.

Before I knew what was happening, he seemed to be living his life without me involved in it. I didn't see him before I went to school, because now he was staying later to finish paperwork, instead of coming straight home in the mornings when he got off. When I got home in the afternoon after class, he would be out somewhere. When I went to my evening dance class, I might see him as he was turning into our street. I would wave, and he would be staring straight ahead as if he didn't even see me.

On Saturday mornings, I would get up early to fix us a nice breakfast, and most times, he didn't even come home until around two in the afternoon. He wouldn't even be tired after being up all night. Then I got the call from the West Indian woman again.

"I'm in love with your husband, and he is in love with me," she said before hanging up.

THROUGH THE FIRE

Boy! She was really pissing me off. I often wished that there was a way to dial a person back that called and hung up on you. Years later, some genius felt the same way and now we have star sixty-nine. Unfortunately, at the time all I could do is pray that the whore would call me back while he was home because so far Michael was lying and saying that he didn't have any idea who was "messing with my head".

Michael had been bragging to some of his single co-workers about what a good cook I was and told them that he was going to have them over one morning for waffles. We set a date and he came home with three airmen. I was in the kitchen fixing waffles, sausage were sizzling on the grill and Michael decided that he had better go to the store; which was three blocks from our house to get more syrup. He could have gone and come back in less than twenty minutes. When he hadn't showed up after forty minutes, I let two of the guys eat, and I went to the store to get the syrup. When I came back, I asked if they had heard from him. They were whispering, snickering, and acting silly. I asked them what was going on.

One of them said, "Well, if you were my old lady, I wouldn't be looking outside for anything. You can take that to the bank."

The other two agreed.

"Are you trying to tell me that Michael is seeing someone?" I asked.

"I ain't saying nothing," he replied.

"Well, you're the one who started it," I reminded him.

107

"You're right. Okay, he may be seeing someone. Ask him. It's either that, or he went to Vermont to get the syrup," he said.

They all laughed, but my face felt as if it were on fire. How could he do this to me? When he got home, the guys had eaten, cleaned the kitchen and been long gone. It was nearly lunchtime.

"I saw an old friend of mine from Brooklyn, and we just got to talking and everything. I went to his house and met his family and I swear, I forgot all about the guys being here," he lied.

"There is a woman that keeps calling here. She has a West Indian accent. She told me that you two are seeing each other. Are you seeing her?" I asked.

He looked me right in the eye and said "No."

It was not long after this that I began to go out with Tootie. I was sick and tired of studying, washing and ironing, cooking and cleaning. I needed to get out and have some fun. Tootie and her husband were having problems, and she was sick of always being at home, just like me. I never knew this, but she was a bit of a flirt. Both of us wore wedding rings, but that didn't seem to matter to any of the guys that we met. I wasn't interested in anyone except my husband, so I didn't pay this one bit of attention. Tootie, on the other hand, was eating it up! When we got ready to leave, this one guy, who had been in her face nearly all evening walked her to the car. I walked ahead of them. I got in, but she stood outside the car near the back talking with him. I couldn't hear their conversation, but I could see them in the rear view mirror. I saw her give him a piece of paper. I didn't say anything to her about it when she got into the car.

We talked about everything except that. I could understand why Tootie would want to have an affair. Her husband was abusive towards her. He wanted her to stay at home and take care of the boys, and the house and nothing else. He didn't even want her to have friends. If he came home while I was there, I had to leave. He would walk in the house, and not even speak to me. Tootie would jump up, grab the broom, and act as if she were cleaning up. I had seen her with many black eyes, and busted lips.

She even told me that he didn't make love to her; he raped her. Seeing her giving this man her number, especially during this period of my marriage, I felt betrayed. I don't know when she began to see Kevin, but I knew that she was seeing him. She would ask me to watch the boys for a couple of hours while she ran an errand. She had never done that before so I knew she was cheating.

One night while Tootie and I were out a man whom we had seen many times before at the club, came over to our table. He introduced himself and told us that the NCO club was going to be holding try-outs for models to be in a fashion show. He asked if we were interested. We decided that we would do it. I knew that it would boost my self-esteem a bit as well as give me something to do with my spare time, since school was out for summer.

109

»CHAPTER 14«

I TALKED TO MICHAEL about it when I got home that evening. He mumbled something about me being overweight. I couldn't believe he would say something like that. I weighed only a hundred and twenty-five pounds soaking wet. However, that wasn't the thing that made my self-esteem drop drastically. One evening, he decided to stay at home. I had took a hot bath, and put on a satin two-piece teddy. I came into the living room with a bottle of champagne that had been in the refrigerator for quite some time, and two chilled wine glasses. We cuddled and then decided to take it up in the bedroom. As we lay on the bed, I asked him what he thought of my lovemaking.

"You mean you want me to give you a grade?" he asked.

"Yeah, something like that," I responded.

He looked off, thinking and then he said, "Well, on a scale of one to ten, I say I'm going to have to give you a two, maybe a three".

I sat up shocked. "A two!" I shrieked.

"Well, what do you want me to say? You don't know anything about oral sex. You never take the initiative and you're not spontaneous. Hey baby, look you asked me," he said seeing that I was hurt.

I was so upset that I got up and went into the bathroom slamming the door loudly behind me. I leaned against the sink looking at myself in the mirror.

"A two!" I said to my reflection. "A freaking two" I kept repeating.

That hurt me deeply. When I came out twenty or thirty minutes later, Michael came into the bedroom where I was now laying across the bed.

"Look, I'm sorry. I didn't mean to hurt your feelings. I would never have said anything, but you asked me," he reminded me.

"Well, you're the big man with all of the experience. Why didn't you take the time to show me?" I asked him.

"I thought that you would eventually pick it up," he said.

I looked at him like he was crazy. Just out of the clear blue sky, he expected me to become this expert lover. I walked out the room and left him sitting there alone. The next time he got some from me, he would appreciate it!

Try-outs began for the fashion show about three weeks later. When Tootie and I got to the NCO club, the line was all the way out to the parking lot. It looked like every black person on Holloman had showed up that day, and a few white guys who thought they were black. We were lead into the restaurant and asked to take a profile and fill it out and have some refreshments.

"Did you think so many people were going to show up?" I asked Tootie.

111

"No, this is crazy!" she said.

After filling out the profiles, we got something to drink and waited to see how this was going to play out. Tootie and I looked up about the same time to see a fine, dark-skinned brother coming towards our table. I leaned in to whisper to her, not realizing that she was leaning in to whisper to me also. Our heads bumped. We started to laugh and couldn't stop. He came over to our table smiling showing the whitest sexiest smile I had seen in quite a while.

"Are you laughing at me?" He asked.

"No, ain't nobody laughing at you. Who are you?" I teased him.

"Oh it's like that? Trying to play a brother? That's cool. Just for that I'm gonna sit right here and bug the hell outta y'all," he said sitting down. He filled out his form and put it in the box with the others. He went to the refreshment table and came back with two plates of food.

"Dang, you're gonna eat all of that?" Tootie asked him.

"If the good Lord's willing and the creek don't rise. What are you guys name?" he asked putting a meatball in his mouth.

"They call me Tootie and this is my girl Toni," she said.

He wiped the barbeque sauce from his lips and held out his hand to me. I took it.

"Toni? That's cool. I like that. You're beautiful," he said smiling.

112

"Thanks. I think you're beautiful too," I said.

It took three or more hours for everyone to finish filling out the forms and getting them reviewed. We each had to walk across the floor, and spin around and walk back out. If they wanted to keep you, you were handed a number and asked to return to your seat. At the end of the afternoon, the crowd of a couple hundred people had been narrowed down to about twenty five women and ten men. Tootie, Leon and I were all picked to be in the fashion show.

We walked out to the parking lot together. He was pulling nervously on his t-shirt, running his hands over his stomach.

"So, you guys take it easy and I'll see you soon," he said looking at me.

When we got in the car, Tootie started teasing me. "Girl, that man wants you!"

"Child, please. You got all of that from what?" I asked.

"Don't even try to act like you didn't see how he was flirting with you," she said. I just smiled because it did feel good that someone thought I was sexy and pretty.

When rehearsals started, I couldn't wait to see Leon again. He always sat with me and Tootie. One evening he invited us to go down town with him to get some Mexican food.

At first, I was going to say no, but I thought about what was waiting for me at home, nothing. I decided to go with him. We rode in his black Camaro. Each time he shifted the gears his hand 'accidently' touched my leg. I could swear that I felt electric shocks!

One evening he and I decided to hook up later and talk. I told him that I would meet him downtown at the zoo. I was very comfortable around Leon. He really listened to me, and took into consideration my feelings. Michael had not talked to me in a long time. I have to know so much about Leon, and I looked forward to rehearsals.

The night of the fashion show, I was so nervous. I think I wouldn't have been so nervous if Michael hadn't been in the audience. Knowing his negative behind was out there somewhere made me just sweaty nervous. We all stood behind the curtain listening to the MC and waiting to hear what the crowd's response was going to be. When we heard the applause, we felt more relaxed.

The show started with two women, both wearing black and white, coming out onto the stage. One walked over to a chaise lounge and lay down. The other sat in the floor in front of the lounge. Teddy Pendergrass' Turn off the Lights was playing. As the lights dimmed, we could see a white dude named Pierre come out and lay down beside the woman on the lounge. He wore only white satin pants and the blond hairs on his chest were glistening. The crowd went crazy!

Tootie had been selected to do a lot of lingerie. I wasn't that confident about my body to be strutting around wearing thongs and garter belts. I did mostly evening and athletic wear. My first number was with Leon. I wore a black silk halter evening dress. He wore a white tuxedo with a black cummerbund. We looked good together, if I had to say so myself. The next

114

number I did with him was with me wearing another evening dress and him wearing a beautiful burgundy suit.

In between numbers, I sipped on champagne that was set up for us and ate chocolate dipped strawberries.

My last number was also with Leon. This time we were to model active wear. I had seen him during the rehearsals in his workout clothes. His body was gorgeous! I wore a black leotard and gold leggings. I was supposed to dance up the runway to She's a Bad Mamma Jamma. I was supposed to turn and walk to the left side of the stage, and then turn and go to the right. Leon was supposed to come onto the stage after I went to the right side of it.

I heard the women going wild screaming, "Come on, baby!" and "Take it off".

I turned to look back and Leon was not wearing what was on the list of outfits. He had put oil on his body and squirted water on his chest and arms to make it appear as if were sweating. He was wearing black wide leg pants with a white waistband with the word "Sam" written across it. Sam is short for Samuels. He walked down the runway moving to the beat of the music. When he walked over to me, he moved his hips from side to side. He put his hands to his waist, moved again, and then, snaps! His pants broke away to reveal him wearing a very tiny red pair of speedos with little white hearts on them. All the women were out of their seats now. He put his arms around me and hugged me tightly.

"Let's knock 'em dead baby!" he said into my ear.

He kissed me passionately, nearly taking my breath away. My first thought was of Michael, and how upset he must be to see Leon kissing me.

After the show, everyone was supposed to hang around the NCO club for a party. I had to go home first because I was feeling a little guilty about Leon kissing me. I knew that Michael was there in the audience, and I wanted to be sure he was cool about the show. When I got home he wasn't there, and it appeared as if he had not been there since we had left for the show. Well, I decided to go back to the party. I changed clothes and took a joint with me. I joined Tootie at her table and she and I danced, drank and partied most of the night. We went to the car and lit up the joint.

"Leon is bad, ain't he?" she asked after a long toke.

"Yes, he is!"

"Did you check out that bulge in his briefs?" she asked.

"I can't believe that you were checking out the man's crotch, girl!" I said laughing.

I secretly checked him out the entire evening. Every time I saw him look in my direction I would smile, and look away shyly.

When I was leaving the ladies room, Leon came up and handed me his phone number. "Call me sometime," he said.

"Yeah, I will," I said nervously. It would be about three months before I got up the nerve to call him.

»CHAPTER 15«

MICHAEL HAD GONE OUT WITH his friends and I had nothing to do. I had been thinking about what he had said about me being a two in the lovemaking department for three months. I was hurt and wrestling with the idea of calling Leon Samuels. I kept thinking about him, and thinking about him. I picked up the phone and called his room.

"Hi Leon, how are you?" I said. He recognized my voice.

"Hey lady, what's up?" he asked. I had lost my nerve.

"Nothing, I thought I would call and say hi," I lied.

"What do you really want?" he asked huskily.

I paused, sighing loudly. "I really want to see you, Leon," I managed to say.

"Tonight?" he asked.

"I guess," I said sounding so silly now.

"You want to see me tonight?" he asked me again. I nodded my head yes, as if he could see me over the phone.

"Tell me that you want to see me tonight. Say, Sam I want to see you tonight," he said. I could hardly catch my breath to say those words. "Tell me that you want to see me," he repeated for the fourth time.

"I want to see you, Leon. I need to see you," I whispered.

"I'll be waiting," he said. I hung up the phone quickly. I couldn't believe that I had finally done it.

I got a magazine from Michael's basket and went into the bathroom. I ran a tub of water and dropped in a couple of bath beads. I went into the kitchen, got a bottle of wine from the refrigerator, and went back to the bathroom. From the window, I could see that we were having a full moon. I laughed nervously about that as I eased down into the bubbles. I took a big sip of wine straight from the bottle and picked up the magazine. I glanced through it and an article caught my eye. I turned the page and began to read it. It was a tale of seduction. The woman in the article was meeting this man at his house that she was planning on seducing. She wore a mink coat, black hose, and black pumps. A pearl necklace was around her neck and pearl earrings in her ears.

After I finished taking my bath, I dried off and put on oil. I wrapped the towel around me and went into our bedroom. I didn't trust walking outside butt naked, anything could happen; however, I wanted something along those lines. I put on a black satin bra and panty set, some thigh hi hose, a pearl necklace and earrings, and got out my full-length blue fox coat. It was nowhere cold enough to wear it. I guessed it to be about forty-five degrees. I put my hair in a French roll and held it there with a pearl hair clip. I checked myself in the mirror and liked what I saw. I put the rest of the wine in the refrigerator and put his magazine back with the others. I got my purse, keys, and left.

Leon answered the door the first time that I knocked. He had on black silk pajama pants, no shirt. His chest was shining, defining his muscular frame. He invited me into the room. I came inside and turned facing him. He locked the door and flicked off the overhead light. A lamp beside his bed illuminated the room.

"Can I get your coat?" he asked.

"Yeah, come and get it," I said.

He smiled and walked to me. He undid the singular button and slipped it down my shoulders. His eyes got big when he saw that I wore only my bra and panties.

"Whew!" was all he could say.

He laid the coat on the spare bed and took a deep breathe.

"So, what can I do for you tonight?" he asked.

"I want you to make me a woman. I want you to teach me how to satisfy a man. I know that you can't do it all in one evening. But if it is okay with you, I'm willing to come back as often as it takes," I said brazenly.

His kisses were different. His touch was different. His lovemaking was most definitely different. When he was finally joining me in this tidal wave of feelings that I was cruising through he did not roll over and go to sleep. I was so weak that there was no way I could get up and go home. I looked at my

119

watch and it was nearly 4:30 in the morning. He saw me look at my watch.

"What time can I see you tomorrow?" he asked. I smiled.

"How do you know that I'll be back?" I asked.

"Your body told me that you'll be back," he said. I liked his confidence.

"I'll be back tomorrow at six," I said.

"No, you'll be back at five," he said between each kiss.

When I finally walked out of there it was seven and people were up and moving around. I saw several people that I knew on my way out of his barracks. I just walked very calmly to my car and left. I knew that if Michael was home he would have a cow. Fortunately, he had not made it home yet. I took a quick shower and was just getting out of the bathroom when he walked in. I didn't even ask him where he had been all night. He thought I was just getting up. I put my coat in the closet and got some sweat pants to put on in the bathroom. I was just stepping into them when I notice the hickey on the inside of my thigh. It was big and nearly purple, no mistaking it for anything else. I put my pants on and went to the kitchen. Michael was in the bed snoring away. I called Leon.

"Did you know that I have a hickey on my thigh?" I asked annoyed.

"Yes, that's my calling card to you. I'll give you a matching one on the other thigh when I see you this evening," he said.

"Leon you can't do that to me. My husband might see it," I said.

"Well, the idea was to keep you from him. You're not going to sleep with him now are you?" he asked me.

"Leon!" I said, just a little bit annoyed. We did meet again that evening. I enjoyed being with him. We talked and got to know each other a little bit. I enjoyed him so much, that I was at his place every day I could get away. Sometimes we just played games; Uno or Simon -- the strip version. Sometimes we went downtown so no one would see us. We rode up to the mountains one Saturday morning. Michael had gone to El Paso for the weekend. He said a friend of his was getting married and he was the best man. I didn't know the guy, so I didn't want to go. Actually, I preferred to be with Leon.

When we got to the mountains, he drove down into the most beautiful valley that I had ever seen. There was a ranch there, and the owners ran a store and had a stocked trout pond in the back of their property. The water was so clear I could see the rainbow trout swimming around. I had never been fishing before in my life. Leon had to put the worms on my hook and took the fish off. We each caught two beautiful fish.

"We're going to eat them now," he said.

"No, I want to save mine. I don't want to eat it," I said.

We walked back to his jeep and rode further up in the mountains. We stopped at a small wooded area and walked through a worn path. We walked holding hands through the woods. We were at the foot of another small lake.

121

"I'm going to get some twigs, you want to help?" he asked.

We walked down to the water's edge. He took the fish out of the cooler I was carrying and packed clay from the ground around the fish.

"What are you doing? I ain't eating that!" I said laughing.

"You'll see. You don't have to eat them. I can eat all of them. But you better not ask for any when you start smelling how good they are," he said pushing me away laughing.

We made a fire with the twigs and laid a piece of mesh wire over the fire propping it up with rocks. We lay the fish over the rack.

"When the clay has completely dried out, the fish are done," he said.

"Is this something that you learned in Basic Training?" I asked.

"No, I saw it on the Electric Company. You remember that show, right," he said.

I hit him with my cap. "You're a nut. You know that right. You're a nut!" I said smiling at him.

"What do you say we do a little something while our lunch is cooking?" he asked nibbling my ear. While the fish were cooking, we enjoyed each other for a few minutes. He removed the rack from the burning twigs and with a knife; he picked the clay open on one of the fish. The meat inside was white and flaky. He took a piece and held it out to me.

"No, after you," I said. He shook his head and ate it.

122

"That is the joint," he said.

I tasted it and it was good. We shared bottles of apple cider and ate the rest of the fish. We had developed a very tight friendship. It went beyond just what we had sexually.

One afternoon, while having a Tupperware party that was going on way too long, the phone rang. It was Leon.

"Hey what's up?" he asked.

That was all he ever had to say.

"Excuse me ladies, I've got to make a run. Barbie, lock up the house for me," I said heading out the door. She came outside behind me.

"This is your party, might I remind you," she said.

"Girl, I've got to see a man about a horse," I said getting into my Mustang.

"And that am I supposed to tell your husband when he comes home?"

"Stay outta my business," I said and drove away.

I had to see Leon. It was a need and desire that I couldn't describe or explain. When he called, I was there. Nothing could keep me from him. I was a junkie and his love was my fix. I didn't want to fall in love him though. I just wanted to be able to kick it with him and be his ace coon boon.

We had been seeing each other nearly five months regularly. This particular evening we were fooling around in his room and I had fallen asleep. When I woke up, he was watching me.

"What are you doing?" I asked.

"You're so beautiful," he said twirling a piece of my hair between his fingers.

I was suddenly uncomfortable. I had seen him watching me like this before, but I had brushed it off. I did not want this man to fall in love with me. He was single and free to do whatever he wanted with whomever he wanted. I knew that I was not leaving Michael, and I just didn't want Leon to be committed to me. I was going to get up and leave but he began to kiss me. He pulled away and sat on the bed his head down.

"What's up, Leon?" I asked.

"Nothing," he said.

He got up and went to the bathroom. The sink was on and he was splashing water on his face. I stood in the doorway.

"Are you falling in love with me, Sam?" I asked.

When I was in a playful mood, I called him Sam. I reached around and put my arms around his waist. I kissed him in the small of his back. He pulled away and walked back into his room.

"Sam, what's wrong?" I asked.

"You need to go," he said annoyed.

"You're absolutely right. This right here is for the birds!" I snapped. I put my clothes on and left.

Two days later, Leon called me.

"I'm sorry about the other day. Can we talk?" he asked.

"Sure, meet me at the park around four," I replied.

"Now!" he ordered.

"I'll be there in ten minutes," I said.

I got my jacket and went to his place.

"I'm falling in love with you. I know that it wasn't part of your plan. I think about you all the time, I can't do anything unless I know that you can share in it with me. I love you," he said. He looked so sad.

"It's not such a bad thing, is it?" I asked.

"Why the hell are you joking with me?" he asked annoyed.

I walked away from him.

"I'm joking about it because I think... because I love you too," I said quietly.

Our lovemaking had always been intense. Now that how we felt was out in the open, it was as if some hidden passion was unleashed. I couldn't get enough of him, and he couldn't get enough of me. As a result, we started to get careless. I was talking to him one night on the phone.

"I've got to study for this exam," he was telling me.

125

"All I need is an hour, or maybe two hours," I said. I didn't even hear the door open.

"You know I know what your one hour is like. You'll get over here and won't want to leave," he said.

"Please Sam. Is it my fault that you're so sweet?" I asked.

Michael reached around me and took the phone out of my hand.

"She won't be over tonight," he said into the mouthpiece and hung up.

He was looking me in the eye. I walked out of the kitchen and into the living room. I went straight to the bar and poured myself a drink.

"Who was that?" he asked. I couldn't say anything.

"Some of my boys told me that you were messing with this dude, a boxer; Samuels or something. When did that start?" he asked. He didn't sound annoyed about it, just weird. I turned to face him.

"A while now," I said.

"A while now? What is that? A week? A month? Three months? What the hell is a while now?" he asked, angrily.

He was very upset now. I took my drink and walked to the couch.

"Please, I don't want to discuss this until you're ready to discuss with me the chick who calls you with the accent," I said.

126

"No, you ain't turning this around! You are going to answer my questions," he shouted.

"No, I'm not. And you're going to get out of my face!"

I snapped. I saw his hand go up. I thought he was going to take my drink. I had no idea that he would hit me. He smacked me right across the side of my head knocking me onto the couch. I was off the couch in one bound. I scratched him in his face. He grabbed my wrists and held me off.

"I can't believe you!" he hissed.

"You got the nerve to ask me about a man, when you've been messing around with this West Indian whore for a year! You can kiss my black behind!" I shouted.

He walked out, letting the screen door slam shut loudly. I picked up the phone and called Leon. I was crying. "Come and get me!" I cried. He was there in less than ten minutes. We went to a park downtown.

"I'm sorry," he said.

He looked at my face. There were no bruises or anything and I told him that it was okay.

"Let's cool it for a couple of weeks. Let this thing settle down. You talk to your husband. You gotta do what you gotta do. What you feel is right. I can't influence you. Okay?" he said.

I went home and waited for Michael. I lied and told him that I broke it off with Samuels. I used that name since that was the only name that he knew. I wasn't sure if he knew who he really was, and I wasn't going to let him get Leon in trouble. In the military, a person could be discharged for adultery if it were proven. After the two weeks, I called Leon and he said that he had given it a lot of thought and it was best if we didn't see each other anymore. I did not think that I could make it without Leon in my life. I couldn't eat. I couldn't sleep. I didn't want to be around my friends or away from the house in case he called. I drove past his barracks each time I did go out hoping to see him. After two weeks, I had to call him.

"Can we go to a movie or something?" I asked. He was silent for several seconds.

"I don't think that would be a good idea. I'll call you back later" and he hung up. That appeared to be the end of our relationship.

»CHAPTER 16«

I WENT ON WITH MY LIFE. I went to school during the week. I studied hard and played harder. I started hanging out at the club so much that folks began to know me by name. I could be walking down the street and people would ask me what was happening at the club that weekend. That was truly pitiful. One reason I did it because I wanted to get the experience to be able to successfully own and operate a night club, which is what I wanted to do when we returned to New York. Daddy was doing very well with the restaurant. He was even talking about opening up another one at a different location in Brooklyn. He had given me hope that I too could one day own a business. I tried to talk to Michael about it, but he wasn't a bit more interested than the man in the moon.

"How are you going to own a business when you ain't worked but one job in your entire life," he asked.

"You are one negative Negro. How old do you think I am? I don't even know why I'm trying to hold this conversation with your stupid behind anyway. You ain't never wanted nothing, and as a result you'll end with just that, nothing," I said and walked away.

I could hardly wait to get a job, make my own money so that I can go on with my life. He was making it very difficult to want to even be around him anymore.

129

Michael had begun to be hostile towards me if I questioned his whereabouts. He was spending more time in the streets than at home. One day, I demanded to know if he was having an affair. I wasn't going to put up with that and he knew that. That was one of the two reasons I had told him I would leave, if he cheated on me, and if he hit me. He promised that he would do neither. He promised me that he would never hurt me. I was crying.

"Please, don't lie to me," I begged.

He adamantly said that he was not seeing anyone. He said that he had been with his friends. I really wanted to believe him so I ignored the doubt that rested just burning away in my heart and I let it go. If he were cheating, I knew that it would eventually come out.

My parents came to visit me that summer, surprising Michael by bringing Brian along. Daddy and Brian had become good friends, hanging out together and even giving him a job in the restaurant. Daddy didn't particular like it out west. He said that it got too dark and it was especially hot that summer. He stayed in the house all day long, not going out for anything until the sun set. Michael was on his best behavior while my parents and Brian were visiting. In the evening, he took them to the pool hall that he said he frequented several times a week. I looked at him sideways. He must have really thought I was a fool. My dad loved Michael and in his eyes, Michael could do no wrong. He put on such a wonderful performance while my parents were out, that he had even convinced me that he was going to change.

130

While eating lunch at the NCO club one afternoon, I learned that they were looking for a hostess for the evenings. All that was required was seating the customers, making sure that the tables were cleaned, and occasionally helping in the bar on the weekends. I applied for and was offered the job. I didn't pay him any attention. When I was paid, I opened up a savings account in my name and banked every dime I made. I tried to learn as much as I could while working in the club. After a year, I had to quit because the people I worked with were getting on my nerves. "I knew you wouldn't follow through on this. If you stop acting like a princess, you might be able to get along with people," Michael snapped.

I wanted to tell him to go take a flying leap into a bucket of monkey piss! I was too tired to argue with him that night.

»CHAPTER 17«

ACROSS THE STREET FROM my house was the Officer's Club. I knew from Barbie that there was an opening for an assistant manager. I really wanted this job because for sure I would get the experience that I needed when I had my own business. I said a quick prayer while the bartender went to get the manager.

I filled out the application at a small table and waited for the manager to come out to interview me.

"Would you like a Coke or Sprite?" A tall, handsome white man asked.

"Sure, a Sprite would be nice. Thanks," I replied.

The ice cubes clicked against the glass as he brought the drink to me. A cherry and lime decorated the drink.

"Good morning, I'm Denver Morgan. How are you?" he said, sitting down holding my application.

I told him about my dreams to one day open my own club. He listened intently as this elaborate lie rolled from my lips about how my father had owned his restaurant for almost twenty years. I lied and said that my mother owned a real estate business in Harlem. My father did own two restaurants, but he had only been in business for himself about three years. My mother worked at a real estate office, she didn't own it. He smiled and nodded looking very impressed. I almost believed the story myself. He slid me a W-4.

"Why don't you go on and fill this out, and then I'll show you to your desk. I wish I could say office, but we're going to have to share one for now," he said standing up.

"I got the job?" I asked surprised.

"If you want it," he said. I was so excited I walked home, forgetting that I had driven the car. Embarrassed, I had to walk back over there and get the car!

I went to the supermarket and got two fat, juicy T-bone steaks to put on the grill and a bottle of wine. Michael was off from work, but I decided not to tell him about the job until after dinner. Michael lit the grill and had the steaks sizzling away. I had a salad in the fridge and was making fries to go with the steaks. When I came inside the kitchen with the platter of steaks, I heard the front door close loudly. I got to the door just in time to see Michael hurrying down the walkway with an overnight bag in his hand. I opened the door to shout for him to come back, but he drove away. I think I saw stars I was so angry. He knew that I had been planning this meal. He had waited until I had gotten busy and fled like a freaking dog. I calmed down and drank a glass of wine. Maybe he had gone to get me a gift, or a card. He had to be coming back, I kept telling myself. I only waited thirty minutes before I called Tootie to come over, eat a steak with me, and celebrate.

After Tootie went home, I called Mommy and told her about the wonderful evening I had planned and how Michael had just up and walked out when my back was turned.

"I'm so miserable, Mommy. I don't understand why he treats me this way. I try to be nice to him and at every turn I make he is standing right there waiting to hurt me," I said.

"Toni, are you sure that he is deliberately trying to hurt you?" Mommy asked.

"Yeah, I'm sure! I told him that I had a surprise for him and that I was cooking steaks. He lit the grill for me. I hate him, Mommy! He takes me for granted and he is a liar. Every time I turn around this West Indian woman is calling me talking junk and Michael swears that he don't know who she is," I said, just fussing.

"Baby, you're going to drive yourself crazy. If things are that bad, why don't you just come back home? You know you are welcome back home. Your father and I will do whatever we can to help you be settled in. I want you to be happy," she said.

I just wasn't ready to leave yet. I knew that my parents would help me to get my own place and whatever else I needed. The thing was that it wasn't their responsibility. I wanted to be able to stand on my own two feet. I didn't want to be a burden. Mommy had to drive all the way from Brooklyn to Harlem every day to her job. She also had to help Grandma Carson now that she was getting older. I didn't want either of my parents to feel that they had to also help me. No, I had to stay and work at the club at least two years. I just had to find a way to tough it out.

I enjoyed working at the club. I had to schedule wedding receptions, retirement parties, birthday parties and promotions. I also was very instrumental in assisting with getting live acts to come to Holloman to perform at the Officer's Club and the NCO Club. I met managers of various artists and was very proud when I was able to get the Temptations to come to perform for us for the Fourth of July Pool Party. Right after they left I was also able to get Reba McIntyre for one of the Captains retirement parties.

When I tried to express my joy with Michael, he acted as if I had said that I had gotten a four-headed lizard to perform.

"Who is Reba McIntyre?" he asked.

"She's a country and western singer, Michael. I know you've heard of her!" I snapped.

You didn't have to be a fan of any particular genre of music to have heard of Reba. Every time we turned on the radio, one of her songs was on. We were in New Mexico; it wasn't like they had a radio station that played soul music. I had gotten used to listening to all kinds of music. He was so narrow minded and ignorant. In order to keep from killing him, I had to find a way to live with him, and ignore his attitude and the fire in my heart.

I didn't have much energy and wanted to sleep all of the time. I thought I was coming down with the flu. I began to take a cold medicine, but didn't feel any better. I took vitamins and though I had a little bit more energy, I still felt weak and dizzy. I finally made an appointment to see Dr. Choi, our family doctor. I was given a blood test, and sat in the lab waiting for the results.

"Well, your potassium is low, so I'm going to prescribe a prenatal vitamin for you to take twice a day. Once in the morning and once at night," he said.

I evidently was only half listening, because he had to repeat if before it dawned on me that he was telling me that I was pregnant.

"I'm going to keep a close eye on you for the first three months. When we make it that far, then I will put you on bed rest so that we can have this baby," he said.

I couldn't wait to get home and call Michael. Half way home, I decided to go to his job and tell him in person. He was so excited that he picked me up and twirled me around, laughing and crying. No one would have guessed that last week we had argued and said evil things to each other.

I was very careful those first three months. I did mostly paperwork at the club, leaving the running around to Denver. I wanted this baby more than anything, but I was dreading four months of bed rest. Mommy told me that she would come out the last three months and stay with me until I had the baby.

Staying in the bed was very difficult for me. Tootie, Barbie and Liz took turns cooking, cleaning and sitting with me. Lying around with nothing to do was driving me up the wall. Michael and I would play board games and card games until I dreamed about them. We watched reruns of The Jefferson's, Good Times, Sanford and Son and Different Strokes. I watched the soap operas until I realized that nothing ever changed in these people's lives.

Michael didn't run out on his day off, instead he stayed home with me. Slowly, the months ticked by. Soon I was in my last trimester and Mommy came out to be with me. By then I had gained nearly eighty pounds. I looked and felt like a big cow.

"Baby, you're more beautiful now than you have ever been," Michael said.

I knew that was a lie. On one of my doctor's appointments, I hurriedly slipped my feet into my shoes only to be teased when I got to the clinic because I had on one blue shoe and one beige one! I knew they felt different, but I thought it was because my feet were probably swollen. Everyone laughed and thought it was so funny, except me. I wobbled to the car in tears.

During this time, Michael went to work, and came home. I watched as he helped Mommy fold the laundry and cook dinner. They painted the baby's room and set up the nursery while I hollered orders from my bed.

"I don't want yellow trim, I want a border! Put up the Winnie the Pooh curtains, and take down the lace!"

"Michael, wake up! Wake up! My water broke!" I was shouting.

He got up from the bed, still half-asleep, spun around and nearly passed out from getting up too fast. He sat on the side of the bed while I got my suitcase and the jeans he had thrown over the shower rod.

"Wake up!" I said right in his face.

"Okay, okay," he said, finally acting like he knew what I meant.

Mommy was running around the house making sure I had everything. We got outside to the car, when she remembered that she had left her partial in a glass beside the bed. She had to go back and get it.

When we got to the hospital, Michael had to fill out some forms, so I was wheeled down the hallway to get ready to have the baby. I was weighed, and my blood pressure was checked. I slipped into the ugly hospital gown and climbed into the bed. By then Michael had joined me.

"Let's do this, Mommy," he whispered against my face as he kissed me.

In the labor room, with him on one side and Mommy on the other, they were about to drive me crazy. Then finally, our beautiful daughter was born. She was laid on my stomach while Michael cut the cord. We were so happy we had a beautiful, healthy baby.

After I was comfortable in my room, Michael went to the nursery to get the baby. I was so tired that I fell asleep watching him whispering to our daughter. When I woke up, he was still holding her. Mommy was laying in the recliner fast asleep.

"You better put her down and let her get some sleep," I said.

"Hey, baby. Look. She has my fingers, but she has your legs. She is so precious," he said.

"What do you want to name her?" I asked.

"Michael. So, I can call her Mikey," he said.

"You must be crazy. You are not going to call my child Mikey.

"What about that name you had picked out. Alexis?" he said.

"No. I was just kidding. I don't like Alexis Carrington that much to name my child after her. I like the name Marissa that you had picked out. Do you still like that name?" I asked.

We decided to name her Marissa Danielle, after his Frat brother Danny.

»CHAPTER 18«

THE NEXT MORNING DR. CHOI and another doctor came into the room.

"Wake up Mommy," Dr. Choi said.

He had a worried look on his face. *Oh, Lord! What was wrong?*

Marissa had jaundice. She was going to be kept under the bilirubin lights until she was better. In the meantime, I wouldn't be able to hold her. Mommy and Michael hadn't gotten to the hospital yet. I called the house, but they weren't home. They were probably on their way to see us. I cried and cried. My poor baby! Later, it was explained to me that it wasn't a life threatening illness. It would have helped if the doctors had told me that when they first dumped this news on me. When we went down to the nursery, Marissa was laying right by the window, butt naked, with cotton balls over her eyes, and a pink hat on her head. All of these people were crowded around looking at the poor little yellow baby with all her butt up in the air for the world to see!

I spoke to the nurse. "Does she have to be at the window for everyone to stare at her?"

"I'll see about moving her away from the window," she answered.

THROUGH THE FIRE

After three days, I had to leave the hospital. I hated to leave Marissa there. I felt just terrible, crying all the way home. I went straight to bed, pulling my blankets all the way up to my ears, and facing the wall.

"Mommy, can you close the blinds? If anyone comes over, I don't want to see them," I said.

I just wanted to go back to sleep. Marissa stayed at the hospital ten days. I would go over early in the morning, and stay until late at night. I was so glad when they had gotten her levels down to normal.

Everyone came by bringing gifts and wanting to see the baby. I had so much to learn about babies. When she cried, I just knew something was wrong with her.

"She's just hungry," Mommy assured me.

Two days after she came home, her cord fell off in the diaper. I began to freak out. I didn't know what had happened.

"It's supposed to come off. Don't get so excited, or you'll make her a nervous wreck, not to mention what you're doing to me!" Mommy joked.

I didn't know what I would do when she went back to New York. I knew that she would be leaving soon, because Daddy was getting lonely.

Two weeks later, we were taking her to El Paso to the airport. "You're going to be just fine. You'll be surprised to see how much comes with instinct," she told me as she began to board the plane. We pushed the stroller through the crowded airport in silence.

"I don't know nothin' 'bout taking care of no baby!" I said to Michael. He just smiled and kissed me on the forehead.

Mommy was right; my instinct kicked in and I was doing a good job of this mothering thing, if I had to say so myself. I always had breast milk pumped and ready to go with me to my errands. I could tell what she wanted from the sound of her cries. I hand washed her clothes and even ironed her diapers. I was becoming a great Mommy! Michael asked to work days and was given the hours he requested. He would get up and feed Marissa during the night, and allow me to sleep. Everything was going so wonderfully. Unfortunately, just as things change, they sometimes stay the same. When I decided to go back to work eight weeks later, Michael decided that he was going to start back working at night, so that he could go to school in the daytime.

"Who's going to watch the baby? You promised to work at night so that I wouldn't have to pay a sitter!" I said.

"Do you really think the world revolves around you? Well, guess what? It ain't about you! There are things that I want to do with my life too!" he snapped.

He totally caught me off guard. If he thought for one minute that my plans were going to change, he was crazy! I called Barbie to see if she could watch Marissa for me while I was at work. I tried to work out a salary to give her, but she insisted she didn't want me to pay her.

I had to get organized now that I had to pack a diaper bag, and get the baby ready before going to work. Since Michael wasn't willing to help out, I decide that I couldn't do everything by myself, and if he wanted to wear a freshly starched uniform every day to work, then he would either do it himself, or put his uniforms in the cleaners. It was hard on me the first couple of months. I tried repeatedly, to find different ways of doing things so that I wasn't burnt out on my days off. One thing that was making it hard on my body was that I was still breastfeeding. I weaned Marissa off the breast milk when she was only four months old. Not having to pump breast milk, gave me back two hours each day, now I could get more sleep.

By now, Michael was totally ignoring me, and I was sick of trying to kiss his behind to make him be nice to me. I still cooked, and cleaned and washed clothes. I still went to the supermarket and dry cleaners and wrote out the checks to pay our bills. Michael went to work, came home when he felt like it, and slept and ate. Then out of the clear blue sky, he decided that we should work on our relationship. I went with him again to a marriage counselor. Since he was re-enlisting, he decided to take a course to see if he could become a Drill Sergeant. Off to Las Vegas he went for eight weeks. He held my hand, kissed me good-bye, and flew off into the wide blue yonder.

»CHAPTER 19«

THAT FIRST NIGHT HE WAS GONE, I invited Tootie and her boys over so we cook on the grill. I had never been alone in a house by myself in all of my life. I was going to enjoy this time. The baby and I spent the days running around having fun and spending time with my girlfriends. On the first Friday night alone, I decided that I wanted to go out and party. I hadn't been out dancing in quite a while. I got Barbie to watch Marissa, and Tootie and I went to the NCO Club. Roger and the Human Body, a band from Ohio was performing that night. The lead singer Roger Troutman was awesome. The group later went on to become the famous band Zapp. They were so good that we went back the next night. Leon was there with his girlfriend. It hurt me to see him with someone else, but he wasn't mine to have. When he went to the bar, I went up to him.

"Hi Leon, how are you?" I asked.

"Hi Toni," he said and walked away, carrying two drinks.

He didn't have to be so funky about it, I thought to myself.

Those eight weeks zipped by so fast and Michael was back home. He stayed home two nights in a row and then he hit the streets.

"Where are you going?" I asked.

"Out with Darryl," he lied.

"Out where?" I pressed.

"I don't know. It depends on what's happening. We might go to the club or we might go to a party. I don't know, Toni. Why the first degree?" he asked.

"I just wanted to know where you were going. You've been gone eight weeks, you would think you'd want to stay home and spend some time with your family," I said.

"Well, I ain't seen my boy in eight weeks either," he replied.

"Go, have fun! Do your thing," I said, and left him alone. No man was going to be shaping up his mustache, putting on cologne, and shining his shoes just to go see another man. He was going to see his whore.

He crept home at 6:30 that morning. I was sitting up in bed feeding Marissa. He couldn't even look at me because he had been out all night whoring around.

"How was the party?" I asked.

"We went to the NCO club and then I hung out with some of the guys from work playing pool at this bar downtown," he lied.

He went to the bathroom and turned on the sink. I watched as he soaped up his face and neck. He saw me watching him and pushed the door shut.

145

"Bastard!" I said under my breath.

I got up and went to living room. I didn't want to be near him. When Marissa fell back to sleep I laid her in her crib and went back to the couch. I woke up around 8:30 that morning. I was fixing breakfast and Marissa whined loudly. She was teething and was miserable. "Could you get up and watch the baby while I fix breakfast. You should have brought your butt home at a decent hour," I snapped.

He got up, got the baby, and went back to our bedroom slamming the door loudly. I sat at the table eating my eggs and bacon alone, and seething. I showered and went downtown to get some information about graduate school. I was told that I would have to go to El Paso to get my Master's degree. That was an hour away. I had promised Daddy that I would finish college and get my degree, and I wasn't going to let him down.

When I got back home, Michael was in the bathtub with Marissa.

"We'll be out in a minute," he said.

I knew he was probably hungry, so I went to the kitchen to fix him a Sloppy Joe and some fries. The telephone rang just as I dried my hands. I picked it up.

"Hello? Hello?" I said.

No one said anything. I knew it was the West Indian woman. I hung it up and went back to the stove. It rang again. I answered it, just as Michael turned the corner with a dripping wet baby in his arms.

"Hello?" I said.

"I love your husband. He loves me. Please, let him go," she said. She was crying, her voice breaking so it was difficult to understand what she had really said.

"What?" I asked.

When she began to repeat it, I handed the phone to Michael and took Marissa from his arms. I carried her slippery body to the bed and laid her down. I was hurting deeply, but I had to go on about my life as if nothing was going on because my daughter needed him, and he needed to be with his child. I wiped my nose in the bathroom and checked myself in the mirror. I oiled my child, dressed her in a yellow flowered onesie and combed her hair. I spread a blanket on the living room floor and lay her on it. While I cleaned the tub, Michael came to stand in the doorway.

"I'm going out," he said.

I watched from the window as he got into his car and sped away. He came home six hours later! I didn't even ask him where he had been. I had decided that I would no longer ask him. I didn't really want to hear him lie to me anyway. However, some things were definitely going to change.

The next morning, I was standing in the kitchen fixing fried eggs and corned beef hash. Marissa was banging a frozen teething ring on her high chair. I heard Michael moving around in the bathroom. I set the table and called him to eat. He came in, kissed Marissa on the forehead and sat down. I poured his coffee into his favorite cup and sat down. He picked up his fork and began to eat, avoiding eye contact. Suddenly he pushed his plate away.

"I ain't never liked fried eggs. Corned beef hash gives me gas like a motha! Your coffee, it tastes like mud," he said calmly.

I sat there speechless. He got up and walked out. At the doorway he looked over his shoulder, "Oh yeah, I've been having an affair with Cynthia Box for the past three years." He walked to his car quickly. I stood at the doorway holding a knife, breathing heavily and thanking God that he walked out before I had time to stab him with it.

When he came back home a couple of hours later, I was watching the Phil Donahue Show.

"I've been driving around thinking about how we can save our marriage. What I can do to make it all up to you. Now I'm asking you what I can do to make it up because I swear I never meant to hurt you," he said acting like he was going to cry.

I turned to look at my husband. He was no longer that skinny young man I'd met in Coney Island who promised me that he would love me forever. I looked at him for a pregnant moment and felt absolutely nothing. He had betrayed me and our child. How could he have done this to me? I had been everything to him, everything a wife and friend could be. I pressed his uniforms and pinned them with his medals every day. I gave his boots a spit shine, ruining my manicure. When he was scheduled to be at work at six in the morning, I was up at four-thirty in the morning, helping him to get ready and fixing his breakfast. I took lunch to him and his partner. If he worked midnights, I would be up helping him to get ready and fixing him dinner. I learned to like basketball and football. I had spent many a Sunday sitting in front of the television cheering for whatever team he was rooting for. I had loved him and cherished him with every fiber of my being. Other couples envied us because we were so close.

Yet, there was something about him that I didn't like, I despised. It caused him to lie when I asked him if he were seeing another woman. For three years, he was sleeping with this heifer and me! My chest began to hurt. I could hardly breathe. My heart had been broken into a zillion pieces. I turned my back to him and cried. I didn't want him anymore. As soon as I got my Master's Degree, I was gone. Once again, I found myself shutting down, and functioning as expected. I would continue to cook his meals, and clean his house. I would even do his laundry. He would have to press his own clothes, and entertain his own friends. There would be no more Sundays of me sitting around wasting five and six hours watching games that I didn't care one way or the other about. I would be civil and give the appearance that all was well. However, I was certainly getting my ducks in a row to move on.

When I awoke the next morning Michael was sleeping on the couch. I instinctively pulled the blanket over him. I stood there watching him sleeping. The more I watched him the angrier I got. Before I took the pillow and smothered him with it, I walked out. I called Mommy when Michael had left to go to work.

"Toni, I can't tell you what to do. That's your decision, but I'll tell you this. A child needs to be with their father, especially a little girl. I believe that we have so many lost young women out here because they didn't have a father or a father figure around them. If you don't want to do it for yourself, do it for Marissa. Try to work it out. Besides, you made a promise before God that you would be with your husband for better or worst. If he is reaching out to you, asking you to forgive him, then you have to try to do that. Don't you think?" she asked.

Wow! I thought she wasn't going to tell me what to do.

I called Leon a couple of days later. I missed him and wanted to see him. He met me downtown by the college and I rode with him in his car up to the mountains. We made small talk, both of us uncomfortable and nervous. After he had parked, we walked down a little path that led to the lake holding hands, and sat down on the ground.

"Do you remember the first time we came here?" he asked. I laughed.

"Yes, I do. We came here to catch some fish. You killed them then wrapped them in mud. But, they were so good, Leon," I said.

"We were good," he said, taking my hand. I could tell he had something he was going to tell me and I would be hurt again. He was looking out across the lake. I could hear him breathing. I wanted him to just say it, and get it over with.

"I'm seeing someone right now. I'm not in love with her, but I think that she is a good person, and I would like to see where it could go. I just want you to know that I am always going to be there for you, okay?" he said. I put his hand to my lips, kissing it.

"Yeah. That's cool," I said. I didn't want him to see me cry, so I tried very hard to hold back the tears.

We sat there for another hour or so and then we headed back to the base. It was over between us. It was too late for us! Oh my goodness! I couldn't bear that thought, that possibility.

»CHAPTER 20«

I DROVE TO TOOTIE'S HOUSE. She always cheered me up when I was down in the dumps. When I got to her house, her crazy kids were running around in their Underoos acting as if they were on a Kool-Aid high.

"I'm thinking about leaving to go back home in about six months," I said.

"Girl, you know you can't leave me here by myself," she said.

"As soon as I get my degree I'm leaving this desert!" I said.

I saw the sad look in her eyes, but I couldn't stay here because of our friendship. I wanted to explain it further, but she started sweeping her kitchen as if I wasn't there. After a few minutes, I got up to leave.

"I'll call you later, okay?" I said.

"Sure! I will talk to you later," she said.

Michael had decided that maybe we should see a counselor again. This would be the third time he brought it up, but this time he seemed to be serious. We went to the doctor's office in his raggedy car. He led Dr. Simon to think that I was cold and unloving. Everything that was wrong in our relationship was because of something I said or did, or didn't say or didn't do. I kept trying to interrupt and give my side of the story. I ended up shouting loudly to get my point across. I only seemed to confirm Michael's accusations that I was difficult. It was so stressful that after we left there I asked him to stop at the liquor store so we could get a bottle of Barbados Black Rum. I cracked it open on the way home and drank right out of the bottle.

After I took a swig of the rum, I handed the bottle to him.

"I ain't made out of the same stuff you are, I have to drink mine with Coke," he said laughing.

"Yeah, you've always been a little sissy when it came to liquor, haven't you?" I teased him. We both laughed.

"I've missed the sound of your laugh," he said.

"I missed you giving me a reason to laugh. You sure managed to make me look like a fool today," I said.

"That wasn't my intentions," he said, trying to hold my hand. I was too busy drinking my rum.

One night at the club things were going pretty slow, so Denver told me that I could either finish up some paper work that he should have done a week ago, or I could hang out in the club and mingle with the patrons. I chose the latter. I played a couple of games of pool with an officer that was visiting from Columbia, South America. I was so glad when it was time to leave because my feet were killing me.

I had just walked inside the house when the phone began to ring. I quickly picked it up so it wouldn't wake up the baby.

153

"I apologize for calling so late. My name is Staff Sergeant Mitchell and I am on duty at Fort Sam Houston army base. We have a patient here named Cynthia Box. Is Sergeant Robinson available?" she asked.

I woke up Michael. He was taking so long, so I asked her to tell me what the problem was.

"Captain Box has been a patient here since she returned from Greece. She has been developing complications with the pregnancy, and last night while performing a C-section she suffered a stroke. The baby is fine, but Captain Box is not. Her blood pressure is dangerously high right now, and we are doing everything we can to get it under control. Someone should get out here as soon as possible. She has Sergeant Robinson listed as the baby's father," she said.

I thought I would pass out. I screamed for Michael to get the phone right this minute. I threw it on the bed beside him. I ran to the bathroom and began to throw up. When I came back to our bedroom Michael was sitting in the floor beside the bed with a stunned look on his face.

"Did you know that she was pregnant?" I asked him. He shook his head, but I could tell he was lying.

"I'll call Denver and see if I can take a couple days off to go out there with you out there," I said. He stood up, running his hands over his head.

"You'd do that?" he asked.

I looked at him and wanted to assure him that I would go with him to the ends of the earth since he was my husband. The
154

truth of the matter was I wanted to see this whore face to face. If she wasn't about to die, I would kill her sorry behind. The next morning, I dropped Marissa off with Barbie and we headed to San Antonio, Texas to face this never-ending drama. I can't remember the ride there, yet we were alone in the car for nearly nine hours. After we checked into Billeting and got a bite to eat, we went to the hospital.

Cynthia laid there, a dark figure with hair almost as white as the sheets, still looking pregnant. There were no tubes or machines that she was hooked up to keep her alive, just an IV. Lucky for her, I thought to myself! I sure would have unplugged them! She seemed to be sleeping peacefully. Michael acted as if he was afraid to come into the room. I wanted to see up close the old heifer that had been harassing me all of these years. She looked awful; her hair wasn't combed, and her lips were chapped and cracked. A nurse came to the door and told Michael that a paternity test needed to be done, and handed him the forms to take to the lab. He held out his hand for me.

"You go on, I'll stay here," I said. He looked alarmed.

"Don't worry. I'm not going to smother her," I said sarcastically.

Actually, I wished that I could and not have to do any time. He reluctantly left with the nurse. I stood there staring at this old, ugly woman who had messed up my marriage. My anger turned to pity as I considered how bad off she was. I went to the bathroom, got a washcloth, and lathered it up with warm water and soap. I began to wash her face and the dried blood on her lips. I rinsed it out and did it again. There was a tube of

155

Vaseline on the bedside table. I squeezed some out and was about to put it on her lips when her eyes suddenly opened. She recognized me and looked frightened.

"Don't get scared. Someone called us and we came to make sure you are all right. How are you are feeling?" I asked.

She still looked afraid.

"Can I put this on your lips?" I asked her since I was standing there holding a big blob of Vaseline on my finger. She nodded her head yes. I gently applied it to her lips, which were pulled down on one side.

"Is Michael here?" she asked.

"Yes. He's taking a paternity test," I replied. She reached up and tried to smooth down her nappy, gray hair. I reached inside my purse and gave her my comb. She was making it worse.

"Here, let me," I said.

My friends would all beat the crap out of me if they knew that I was combing the hair of the whore that slept with my husband, so that she could look half way decent when he came back.

"Thank you," she mumbled.

"Have you seen the baby?" I asked her.

"No, what about you all?" she asked. I knew she really meant just Michael.

"How about I go and get him for you?" I said. I had to get out of there.

I walked down to the nursery to get her son. I could have picked him out with no problem. He looked just like Marissa did when she was born. The same nurse that came to get Michael to take him to the lab wheeled the baby over to the window.

"Can he see his mother?" I asked.

"She needs to get a little stronger before she can hold him," she said.

As I was turning the corner to Cynthia's room, I heard the announcement on the intercom,

"Code Blue Room 345, Code Blue Room 345!" That was her room. I ran up the hall but was barred from entering the room.

No, this is not happening! I thought. This cannot be happening! This woman had better not die! I stood out in the hall, waiting and listening as they worked on her. However, in my heart of hearts, I knew that she was dead.

A nurse had some papers that Michael needed to sign. I went to see the Red Cross Representative, because I wanted to know what was going to happen now. I knew that Cynthia supposedly only had one living relative, because Michael had told me that, but I wasn't going to start believing anything that he said now. I wanted to inquire if there was a mother, or an aunt or somebody around that would raise the baby. Unfortunately, she had no one but an old uncle who lived in Haiti.

157

We walked back to Billeting in silence. Michael tried to reach out and hold my hand, but I pulled away looking at him as if he had two heads. If he felt anything, sadness, or love for this woman, it did not show on his face. He acted very detached from it all. What a cold-hearted man, I thought to myself. When we got to the room, he shut the blinds and turned on the television. In less than thirty minutes, he was knocked out sleep. I tried to get some rest, but he was snoring so loudly I couldn't concentrate. I decided to call Mommy. I went down the hall to the pay phone and called her.

"Toni, I never wanted to have to tell you this, but I went through a similar thing with your father," she said.

"What?" I asked shocked.

"Right after your father moved into my house, a woman from Harlem called to tell me that she was pregnant with his baby. When I asked Clyde about it, he denied it at first. This trick kept calling me and calling me. She had the baby, and your father sent her a money order every single week for two years. But don't you know that baby died right after it was born. He didn't know this, because he never went up there to check it out. He just kept sending her those money orders. Girl, I was so mad with that woman and your father. I think I was more upset with him because he allowed her to make a fool out him. He thought he was protecting me, but I could handle myself. Even after he found out, don't you know that trick started calling me and telling me that Clyde was with her, and he would be sitting right beside me? I was determined that I was not going to let this woman destroy our family and our marriage. After we got our stuff worked out then, you came to live with us. I felt like you had been through enough already and I wanted our home to be grounded, solid. I say all of this to tell you that if you love your husband then work it out. If you don't love him anymore, you don't trust him anymore, you will be miserable if you stay with him just because of Marissa. The Bible tells us that God made only one provision for a divorce, and that's adultery. He broke his marriage vow to you, and you do have the grounds for a divorce if that is what you want. Whatever your decision is, baby, I am here for you", Mommy said.

"That's why I love you so much," I said crying.

"Try to get some rest and call me tomorrow," she said.

As I was walking back into the room, the telephone was ringing. I hurried over to pick it up.

»CHAPTER 21«

MRS. ROBINSON, THIS IS Felicia from the pediatric ward. I don't want to sound like I am prying into your life, but if you all are planning to take a baby home I think that you should bond with him. He is over here crying his little heart out. He needs a mommy, not a nurse," she said.

I sighed and agreed to come over.

All of the babies were in with their mothers when I got to the nursery, leaving Cynthia's baby in there by himself. I washed my hands and put on a green gown.

"What's the matter? You've chased all of the other babies out of here. Are you hungry?" I asked, as I prepared a bottle for him.

I sat down in the rocker and began to feed him. He sucked greedily on the nipple. A nurse came over to kneel beside me.

"I hope that I didn't upset you. I know this is a terrible mess that you're in. I just wanted you to know that I'm praying for you to make the right decision about the baby," she said.

"No, I'm not upset. You're right, if we are going to take him home, he and I do need to bond," I said.

"I think he is a handsome little man," she said smiling.

160

"He looks just like my daughter. She's eight months old. I just weaned her from breast feeding so I could get some rest," I said.

"Well, you might be able to get your breast milk stimulated again if you would like to breast feed him too," she said.

"No way!" I said laughing.

"Well, if you change your mind, I can get you in touch with the LaLeche representative," she offered.

While I was feeding the baby, Michael came into the nursery. The baby had spit up on his t-shirt and I was putting a clean one on him.

"What do you think we should name the baby?" I asked Michael as we were giving him a bath.

"How about Michael Jr.?" he asked.

"How about something else?" I snapped.

"What?" he asked.

"Suppose we have a son? We won't be able to name him Michael because your lover's child already has that name," I said. He made me sick!

"Okay. Whatever!" he said.

"What about Travis? That's a nice name," I said now feeling like a heel.

"Travis is nice. Do you like the name Travis? Huh, do you?" he said to the baby.

On the ride back to New Mexico, I tried not to think about what my friends would say when they hear that I had decided to raise Cynthia's baby. They would all think that I had lost my ever-loving mind. I honestly felt that I had no choice. This baby had nothing to do with how he was conceived. He needed a home, and we were in a position to provide that for him. What Michael thought of me didn't enter my mind until much later.

As we pulled onto our street, Michael wanted to stop and get Marissa from Barbie's house before we headed home. "No, lets' go home and I'll get her after we get settled in," I said. Actually, I didn't want Barbie to be the first to know that Travis was with us. She would get on the phone, call everyone else, and dog me out before I had a chance to explain.

I walked to Barbie's house to pick up Marissa. It gave me a chance to get my speech together if she asked any questions about why we were in San Antonio. To my surprise, she didn't pry. I thanked her for taking care of my baby and pushed her stroller out into the bright sunshine. I prayed to God that I was doing the right thing and that if I am doing the right thing, to help me to bear up under this particular trial.

Travis was lying in the middle of our bed sleeping. I sat Marisa on the bed and showed her the new baby. I knew she didn't understand what I was saying, but she looked at him with curiosity and touched him on the leg.

"Baby," I said.

162

She tried to repeat it, "Ba-ba."

I called Denver to let him know I was going to be in to work that night. "If you need to take a couple more days off, that's cool," he said.

I assured him that I would be there. I needed to get back to work, to get out of this house, and to get away from Michael's expressionless face.

When I arrived to work that night, everyone there seemed to already know that Cynthia Box had died and that I had allowed my husband to bring his love child into our home. I got nothing but pitiful or angry stares from women that entire night. When Denver and I were alone in his office, he shut the door and leaned back in his chair. That was always my cue that he had something that he wanted to say that was hard for him.

"Toni, don't worry about the whispering and stares. That pretty much comes with the territory when you do something out of the norm. And you have to admit that what you did, bringing this baby into your home, is out of the norm," he said.

I was and had been near tears for years because of Cynthia Box and my husband. I started to cry. Oh, I sobbed like a big baby that night. Denver sat right there, leaning back in his chair waiting for me to stop before he said anything else. I was so embarrassed that I wished the floor would open up and swallow me whole.

"Dang girl, you sure do get all ugly in the face when you cry. Good gracious sakes!" he said, laughing. I started to laugh too.

163

He got up, locked the office door, came to my desk, and sat down on the corner of it. "Toni, I'm just joking with you. I didn't mean to make you cry. I admire you. You are one awesome woman. I may be out of line for saying this, but your husband doesn't give a crap about how wonderful you are. He doesn't care that your heart is so big and you are so caring that you are willing to raise another woman's child. And not just any woman, the woman he had an affair with for what three or four years. I've seen this situation a couple of times. Get out of this relationship while you still have this big, loving heart, or else you will grow cold and never really love again," he said softly.

I looked at him and saw that he was truly sincere. I stood and kissed him on the cheek.

"Thanks for caring Denver. I really appreciate it. You're so right," I said.

164

»CHAPTER 22«

WHEN I GOT HOME, it was nearly three in the morning. Michael was in the kitchen walking back and forth with Travis, who was crying his little heart out. He handed him to me mumbling something about him having gas and went to bed. I turned on the light over the stove and turned off all of the overhead lights. I wouldn't go to sleep with a bright light shining in my face from a chandelier that held eighteen bulbs either. I held Travis with one arm while I poured him a bottle of milk. While it heated on the stove, he stared at me, wondering who I am, no doubt. I sat in the recliner and turned on the television. Travis continued watching me as he drank his milk hungrily.

"What are you thinking? What is it that you would like to tell me? Huh?" I asked him.

He finally closed his eyes and went to sleep. I laid him in his crib and went to bed.

Michael got his schedule at work changed so that he could work days and I would take care of the babies. He would take care of them at night while I was at work. It was difficult at first finding time to get to sleep with a newborn in the house and an eight month old that wanted to be up playing and exploring and learning how to walk. I was in control, as usual and was able to work out a schedule that would benefit all

165

involved. When I got home in the wee hours of the morning, Michael was always up walking the baby with the house lit up like a Christmas tree. I finally was able to reach him through all of the "I know how to take care of babies" crap, and get him to see that if the lights were dim, and he just stopped walking and sat down and rocked Travis, he would go back to sleep. However, if he got in the habit of someone flicking on bright lights in his face, and pacing with him, that will be the only way that he will be able to get to sleep. When Michael caught on to this, I would come home and find them asleep, or in the recliner getting ready to go to sleep.

At nine, Barbie came and took Marissa and Travis back to her house, allowing me another two hours of sleep before I felt rested enough to get up and start my day. When the babies took a nap, I did too. I usually was awake before they got up, so I might do a load of laundry, or sweep and mop the kitchen. When Michael got home from work, I took another nap before getting ready to go to work at eight in the evening.

When Travis was about a month old, I was in the commissary with him in his stroller. As I came into the store, I saw two African American female officers standing near the fruit section. They both stopped talking and stared at me.

As I passed them I heard one of them say, "That's her. That's that fool that set us back two hundred years!" I was shocked and hurt.

"Excuse me! Do you have something to say to me?" I asked her.

"No, I don't have anything to say to you," she backed down.

166

"Are you sure, because I thought I heard you say that I set women back two hundred years. Perhaps you would like to explain to me what I did that set us back," I said standing my ground.

"You heard wrong," she said. I walked away looking over my shoulder at her.

My face was burning from embarrassment. I didn't even get the things that I needed from the market. I just walked right out of there and went home. I shut the blinds and sat in the floor with Travis, holding him and trying to understand why someone would be that nosy to get all up in my business and voice such an awful opinion about me when they didn't even know me.

Had I been more alert, I would have seen that even my girlfriends were acting strangely. I was working so much at night, and sleeping so much in the daytime, that I didn't have a lot of spare time to be with them. When I was with them, I just didn't notice that they too were tripping. I didn't notice until Barbie told me that she couldn't watch the babies anymore without being paid. I reminded her that I had offered to pay her when I first had her keeping my children, but she had refused money.

"Well, things have changed now," she said.

"What's changed, Barbie?" I asked.

"You've changed," she replied.

"How have I changed?" I questioned.

167

"You're allowing Michael to make a fool out of you and use you," she said. Perhaps, but what did that have to do with her wanting to charge me for watching my babies?

"I'm not going to make it easy for his sorry ass. That's your job!" she snapped.

"Okay," I grabbed my children and walked out.

Later that evening, I went back to her house and left a check for two hundred dollars under her door. The next day when she came to pick up the babies, I gave a check for four hundred dollars for watching them the rest of the month.

"Now, you're tripping. I don't need all of this money. The money you left yesterday is enough," she said.

She left the check on the television and walked out pushing the stroller down the block like someone was chasing her.

I was upset to the point that I knew that only Tootie could make me feel better. I stopped by her house one evening when I had a late dinner break. She was feeding her sons dinner. We sat in the living room sipping rum and Coke. I told her about Barbie.

"Well, you shouldn't even be surprised. She was never really your friend anyway. But she was right about one thing," she said.

"What is that?" I asked, already knowing the answer.

"That Michael is making a fool out of you," she said. I didn't say anything.

"You know folks are talking about you all over this base, right? Yeah, the women are talking about how crazy you are because you didn't go off on nobody. Didn't nobody get cut up, or beat up. All of the fellows are like; yeah Rob has it going on. He can cheat on his old woman, knock up a whore, bring the baby back home, and let his woman raise it. He's the man!" she said laughing.

I stared at her angrily, trying hard not to curse her behind out. "Do you think I'm crazy too?" I finally mustered up the energy to ask.

"No, I don't. If you had come back without the baby, then I would have thought you were crazy. Toni, what you did, I knew you would do. I wasn't even surprised. But they don't know you like I do," she said softly. She got up and sat next to me on the couch. "Go ahead, cry if you want to. You don't always have to hold it together," she said.

I laid my head on her shoulder and cried.

When I got to work, Denver gave me some paper work to do for an upcoming wedding. That kept me in the back most of the night. Around two that morning I came into the club. I got a Coke from the bar and sat down to listen to Yvette sing. Her set would be over in about fifteen minutes. As people began to leave she motioned for me to come up on the stage while she packed up her things.

"Well, if it ain't Mrs. Robinson", she said as she kissed me on the cheek.

"Hi, Yvette," I said.

169

DARBY WEST

"I was hoping that I would see you before I left. Don't you let these crazy folks meddle all in your business. You did what you felt was the right thing to do. For the baby, it probably was the right thing. It may not have been the right thing for your husband, 'because he is not going to appreciate it. But you did do the right thing bringing the baby into your life and giving him a home. Get your affairs in order. Captain D tells me that you do an excellent job running this club. Finish your degree, take this experience and take your butt back to New York. You can open up your own restaurant and club. Raise them babies. Someone out there will love you like you need to be loved. Now look at that, I just got in your business too!" she said laughing.

I kissed her and went back to work.

I lay in bed that night thinking about my future and that of these two children. I didn't want either of them to grow up thinking that the way we were living right now was normal for a family. I wasn't raised that way. My father and mother were very loving towards each other, and showed it. Michael and I only talked when we had to, or if it concerned the children. Other than that, we had no communication. I didn't want him anymore, and he evidently didn't want me. It was time to go. When I told him that I wanted to return to New York and open up my restaurant and nightclub, he looked at me like I was dreaming some impossible dream.

"Toni, why don't you teach school, or go into real estate or something?" he asked.

"That's not what I want to do. I want to open a restaurant and a club," I replied.
170

"But you don't have any experience!" he said loudly.

"Excuse me! I have worked in a restaurant and club for four years!" I said.

"Working for someone is different from working for yourself!" he said.

"Let me get this straight. Even though I have four years of experience in a restaurant and club, it doesn't count because it wasn't my restaurant and club?" I asked.

"Yeah, that's exactly what....*NO*, that's not what I mean. You didn't even like working at the NCO club. You quit after a year," he said.

He was getting ready to say something else, but I cut him off.

"You know what. I was only telling you that I am leaving. I am not going to sit here and go back and forth with you, because you don't even have a clue as to what you are saying. You're stupid! You're ignorant. And you have no ambitions of your own. I am going back to New York," I said angrily and walked out leaving him sitting there looking like the fool that I thought he was. I refused to discuss this with him again.

I wanted to see Leon before I moved back home. I knew our paths would probably never cross since we were from two separate states, me in New York and him in Pennsylvania. He had been constantly on my mind anyway since I had returned from San Antonio with Travis. I dialed his number when Denver left the office. It was nearly eleven p.m. on a Friday night. The phone rang four times before he answered. I was getting ready to hang up.

171

"Hello?" he said coming out of his sleep.

"I'm sorry. I didn't mean to wake you up," I said.

"Hello Toni. God! It's good to hear your voice," he said, sounding so very good.

"It's good to hear your voice too. How are you?" I asked.

"I'm fine. How are you? I heard you were about to return to New York soon," he said.

"Can I see you before I leave?" I asked.

"If you left without saying good bye, I would have to hunt you down," he said laughing softly.

"What about tonight?" I asked.

"What time is it?" he asked.

"It's eleven. But I don't get off until eleven-thirty. If that's too late, we can make it for another…" I started to say.

"Tonight is fine. See you in a little while," he said.

I hung up the phone trying to contain myself. "I'm just going to say good bye to an old friend. Okay, an old lover. But I would never forgive myself if I left and didn't say bye. Tell the truth! You want to feel his arms one last time. You want to taste his sweet lips…"

"Toni, who are you talking to?" Denver suddenly entered the office.

"Nobody," I blurted embarrassed. He frowned, picked up some papers from his desk and left, looking at me like I was crazy.

"Michael, I'm going to be late getting home," I said hoping that he wouldn't ask me why.

"Sure, okay. Everybody is asleep and I just got out of the shower. I'll see you later, bye," he said.

I ducked into the ladies room and brushed my teeth, freshened up my makeup and combed my hair. I checked myself in the mirror and then sprinted to the car.

"Good night, boss lady!" someone from the kitchen staff yelled out in the darkness, startling me.

"Good night!" I yelled back.

I drove downtown to Leon's new apartment trying hard not to break the law. I hadn't talked to him in over a year. We had seen each other a zillion times, but we only smiled and kept walking.

I rang his bell and waited. He opened the door and stepped back letting me in. I hugged him.

"Did you lose some weight? You look good, girl," he said leading me to the couch. I turned around so he could see the whole effect.

"Yeah, I lost about twenty-five pounds," I said. "You look real good," he said, sitting down. I sat next to him and smiled.

It was so good to see him. "Want a beer? You better say yeah, I went out and got some Heineken," he said.

"Yeah, thanks," I said.

"Do you know about the baby," I asked.

"Everybody knows about the baby, Toni," he said.

"I had to give him a home, Leon. He's just a baby. He didn't have..." I said.

"Hey! Hey! I know you Toni. You have to do the right thing. I wasn't even surprised when I heard that you brought the baby back with you. I just hope that your husband appreciates you," he said.

"Leon, I know everybody and their momma has something to say about me, Michael, the baby and Cynthia. Only a couple of people's opinions mean anything to me. Your opinion matters to me. What do you think? Do you think I did the right thing?" I asked. He took the beer from my hand and sat it on the table.

"Toni, from the moment I laid my eyes on you at that fashion show three years ago, until the last night I made love to you, I thought you were remarkable. Nothing you've done has changed that. Nothing you can do can change that. I just don't want you to get hurt," he said.

He leaned forward and kissed me on the cheek. "I want you to be happy," he said.

"Do you know the other reason I came by tonight?" I asked.

"Why don't you tell me," he said.

"I want you to make love to me tonight like it is our last time together." And that's exactly how he loved me.

When I got home that morning, Michael was sitting in the recliner with Travis on his stomach, watching television.

"How's it going?" I asked.

"We're just watching Saturday Night Live," he said.

"Let me have him. You go to bed," I said.

He got up from the recliner and caught me by surprise with a kiss on the cheek before going to bed. I lay down on the sofa, pulled the blanket up over Travis and me, and turned off the television. I fell asleep with Leon on my mind.

I spoke to an attorney about adopting Travis and started the ball rolling. I called to see about getting tickets for our flight back to New York. Mommy and Daddy were glad that I was coming home. I couldn't wait to get back to the Big Apple. I knew that nothing but wonderful things awaited me and the children. I looked at Michael each day wondering what was going on inside of him, but not caring.

One Saturday afternoon, after both babies had been laid down to take a nap; I went out to the backyard where he was changing the oil in his hoopty.

"Michael, were you ever in love with Cynthia?" I asked. He came to sit with me on the step.

"I was in lust with her," he said.

175

"Explain to me what you mean. How did you and her get together?" I asked.

"Do you remember her from the housing office when we first applied for base housing? That's how we met. After that, it seemed that everywhere I went there she was. She was older than me. I think she was about fifteen years older than me, so we didn't run in the same circles. She was also an officer, and she shouldn't have been fraternizing with an enlisted man. She was aggressive, very aggressive. You and I were having some problems and I thought I could talk to her about them, get some advice on how to make you happy. We used to talk for hours. One thing led to another and the next thing I knew, we had an affair. I was hurt and embarrassed at first but I couldn't stay away from her. I would be out shopping for groceries and then think of her and leave my cart right there in the aisle. I would be playing ball with my boys, think of her, and have to leave the game. It was like voodoo or something. I wasn't in love with her though, I was in lust. I loved you, Toni. I'm just not good for you anymore. You had your dreams and plans laid out when you got here. You jumped right into going to school. You got a job in the field that you were interested in. You were like up here somewhere, and I was down here. I began to resent you for that. I was the one that was supposed to go to school. I was going to be a dentist. I haven't done anything to make my dream a reality. You did it. Everything that you wanted to do, you did. I should be proud of you, but I don't feel anything but resentment. I'm sorry. My head is just messed up right now. Everything is spinning out of control almost. Just when we started working on our marriage, Cynthia had the baby. Then she died and we have the baby now. You're working when I'm

176

home and you're home when I'm working. We're not working on anything together. We're just going through the motions. We're been married almost seven years. That's a long time to throw something away. You know," he said wiping a tear from his eyes, and leaving a black oily smudge on his face. Instinctively, I reached up to wipe it away."

I probably should have called it quits when I first got the phone calls from this woman. I thought to myself. That's when I stopped loving him. The only good thing that came out of me staying with him was Marissa...and Travis. What a mess we were in. I did have sense enough to know that there was a solution to this problem.

»CHAPTER 23«

MY PARENTS WERE GLAD THAT I was coming back home. Daddy had just purchased two more brownstones. He was having them renovated to the original floor plans. I couldn't wait to see their new home. I couldn't wait to get started with my new life!

Tootie and I made plans to get together for dinner before I left to go back home. We made plans to get together at the club on the night that Peaches and Herb were performing. We sat in the restaurant eating our appetizers and talking.

"So, what am I going to do without you now?" she asked.

"We will stay in touch. I'll call you at least once a month. We can also write letters and send pictures. You're my girl!" I assured her.

"Are you going to see Leon before you leave?" she asked.

"Did that!" I said.

"You ho! When were you gonna let me know?" she asked.

"Could you stop talking so loudly?" I asked. I worked there, and didn't want these folks up in my business.

"When did you see him?" she whispered.

"I went to see him about a week ago," I said putting a big piece of steak in my mouth.

"Did you sleep with him?" she asked me just as the server put a basket of fresh bread on our table.

"Could we talk about something else?" I asked, annoyed.

"I want to talk about this!" she said.

"Well, guess what, I don't! So could you please just shut up?" I said.

She continued eating, not saying one word.   After twenty minutes of silence, I asked her what was wrong.

"Ain't nothing wrong. You told me to shut up, so I'm shutting up," she replied.

"This is my last week here, so save the drama," I said.

"Cool!" she said and continued eating her dinner.

I changed the subject, "Don't let me forget to get you my psychology book before I leave. I hope you get Dr. Phelps. He's real good," I said.

"I'll keep that in mind," she said.

I was getting pissed off now.   Tootie and I had been best friends, like sisters for almost seven years.   We had been through thick and thin together.   There nothing that I wouldn't do for her, and vice versa.   I didn't want us to spend out last night together sitting here acting like kids.

"I'm sorry if I hurt your feelings," I said.

"Apology accepted," she said and continued eating her steak. Her attitude still hadn't changed.

"Is Ricky excited about starting first grade?" I asked.

"Yeah," she said.

"Tootie, knock it off, okay," I said.

"Okay!" she said. The server came to clear our plates and bring our dessert. I ate my chocolate cake and picked up the check.

"You take it easy. I hope you enjoy the show," I said getting up. I didn't need this crap tonight. I would pay for the meal and let her see the show, after that screw her. Our friendship must not have meant much.

"Oh girl, sit your behind down. I'm just tripping. I'm the one that's sorry," she said with tears rolling down her cheeks. I slid across the booth and put my arm around her.

"What's wrong?" I asked.

"I'm just gonna miss you and I wish that you were not going. What am I supposed to do without you?" she said crying.

"Oh Tootie, please don't cry. We will always be in touch. I am only a phone call away," I assured her. We sat there until she had calmed down, and then we went into the club to hear Peaches and Herb.

180

I was so busy planning the move, and getting things organized I didn't even think about the impact leaving would have on my friends or me. I would miss Tootie too; however, I had my mother to help me out. Tootie didn't have a relationship with her mother. Besides me, she didn't have any friends. I promised myself that I would make it a point to call her at least once a week, write her often, and send pictures. When I could, I would go back and visit her.

The day finally arrived for me and the babies to leave. I got up that morning filled with so much anticipation. I sat the babies in their high chairs and prepared them some eggs and toast for breakfast. Michael came into the kitchen and kissed Travis on the cheek. He was trying to feed himself and had eggs smeared all over his face.

"I want what he's eating," Michael said laughing.

"Are you going to miss us?" I asked.

"I'm going to miss Marissa and Travis," he said laughing, but I knew he was serious.

He pulled me to him and tried to kiss me. I immediately tried to remember the last time that he had kissed me, or that we had made love. It had been at least two years. He had to have another woman in his life by now.

After putting both car seats in the car and our luggage, we drove to the airport in El Paso making small talk.

"I sure am going to miss the mountains and Mexican food," I said.

"You're not going to miss me?" he asked. I couldn't even think of an answer for that, so I just let it go.

As we walked through the airport with the babies in a double stroller and carrying two car seats, I began to feel antsy. I wished that I had been able to see Leon again.

"So, this is it," Michael said.

"Yep!" I replied. He put his arm around the back of the seat and kissed me on the cheek. I was very uncomfortable with the sudden display of affection.

"Toni, don't write me completely off yet," he said. I looked up and saw Leon standing by the ticket counter. Michael turned to see who I was looking at.

"I have to say good bye to him," I said to Michael. I wanted to run into Leon' arms, but I didn't. I walked as calmly as I could to him.

It was obvious that he had been crying. He held my hand tightly as we stood there looking into each other's eyes. We walked away from the gate and went to a nearby bar. He pulled me to him and kissed my eyes, my lips, my throat, and my hands.

"Do you love your husband?" he asked.

"Leon…" I said.

"Toni, I want to know if you are staying with him because you love him or because of the babies. That's all I'm asking you." He said.

182

"I…" I said.

"I love you, Toni. Please answer me," he said.

"I'm not staying because of Marissa and Travis," I said.

He shook his head.

"Let me tell you how much I love you. I have to have you. I need you in my life. I can do right by you. You have to give me this chance, Toni. I can be there for you and fifty babies. I cannot let this go. I've been trying for three years. It hasn't worked," he said.

"My plane is boarding, Leon," I said crying.

If it's meant to be, we will be together," he said kissing me good-bye.

Michael stood up when he saw me. "What are we doing, Toni? I saw the way you looked at him. That's the way you used to look at me, but you don't anymore. If you love this man, tell me baby. I'll have to let you go," he said.

I hadn't really looked at Michael in a long time. He had gray hair around his temples. When did that happen? Deep furrows lined his forehead. We were not the same people we were twelve years ago when we met on Coney Island. There was nothing to hold onto anymore. Neither Marissa, nor Travis would be enough. I knew that, and he knew that.

"We'll talk when I get to New York," I said and boarded the plane carrying a car seat in each hand. The babies slept most of the way there. When the pilot announced that we were flying over DC, Travis woke up. I took him out of his seat and fed him a bottle. He loved to look at me, studying my face. He always looked at me like he had something to say.

"What? You want to tell me something? You love me? That's what you want to say? Say it then," I said to him. I kissed him on the lips and he threw his head back and laughed.

»CHAPTER 24«

DADDY WAS WAITING FOR US at the airport. "Where is Mommy?" I asked.

"She had to go and check on Momma Carson this morning. She hadn't gotten back when I left. I know she has a Bible study at one o'clock. She ought to be home by the time we get there if all is going well. Look at these babies!" Daddy said kissing each of them.

As we made our way down to the luggage claim area Marissa banged on her stroller tray.

"She's hungry. I can't wait to get home," I told Daddy.

"Well, in a little while that's where you'll be," he said. We got our luggage and walked out into the bright New York sun.

"Oh, I've got a surprise for you," Daddy said as we made our way to the parking deck. Daddy had just gotten a brand new wine colored Cadillac.

"Daddy, it's the joint!" I said.

"It's pretty sharp, ain't it? It drives like butter. Smooth!" he said laughing.

As we drove down Atlantic Avenue, I looked out of the window. The city seemed to have changed, but I know it didn't. I had changed. I had gotten the opportunity to leave New York for a little while and I have come back home. I was ready to take my bite out of the Big Apple.

When we turned onto Lafayette Street, and I saw the outside of the two new brownstones that my parents had purchased, I was overjoyed. Daddy's restaurant, Clyde's Place was within walking distance.

Mommy wasn't home when we got there. We took our luggage upstairs and put the babies on the floor to play. Marissa was walking and getting into everything. She was especially impressed with the brass and glass enclosed fireplace. Her favorite word was "No!"

I called Michael to let him know that we had made it to New York safely, but he wasn't home. I couldn't believe that he was not home when he was supposed to be off work that day. His family was up in the air for seven hours, you would think he would stay home long enough to make sure we got to New York safely. I left a message on the answering machine when it came on.

When Mommy got home, she just hugged and kissed the babies until Marissa was stamping her feet and shouting "No!"

"She's a mess, ain't she?" Mommy asked.

"No. She just likes the way that word sounds," I said.

We walked up the block to the restaurant and had dinner. It was a very nice place. "Daddy, I am so proud of you," I said.

"Well, I want to show you something when we leave here," he said.

Around the corner from his restaurant was a vacant building that used to be a jazz club and restaurant. It was exactly what I had in mind.

"I'm checking into getting it for you. I already gave them a bid. I'm just waiting to hear back from the owners," he said.

"Wow!" I said. It was my club. I saw me in there. It was mine!

"Clyde how do you know she wants this place? Give her a chance to be settled in. My goodness," Mommy said.

Oh, but I did want this place. I wanted it so badly that I could see me actually running it. I just smiled and patted Daddy's hand. We knew the deal!

At ten o'clock that night, Michael called to let me know he had just gotten my message.

"Where were you?" I asked.

"I decided to go on to work so I could have the weekend off," he lied.

"Do you want to say hi to Marissa? She's running around here like a wild woman. My parents think she has no home training. Hold on, let me get her," I said.

Marissa loved to talk on the phone. "Hello." she said into the mouthpiece. I don't know what Michael was saying to her, but her lip was poking out and she was about to cry, so I took the phone.

187

"Listen, it's late and we are all tired. I'll talk to you on the weekend." I said.

"Okay, take care," he said.

"You too," I said and hung up quickly before he lied and said 'I love you'.

I called Leon next. We talked on the phone over an hour. I wanted to assure him that Michael and I were not together. Our marriage was over. I wanted to be with Leon, but I was afraid to say that right then.

"I love you," he said before hanging up.

"I love you too," I replied.

I slept like a baby that night. The babies slept well too! We didn't wake up until daybreak. I carried Travis downstairs to get him some milk. Mommy and Daddy were still asleep. I decided to fix breakfast for them. By the time that I had finished everyone was up and stirring. Daddy and Marissa came into kitchen with a Pamper.

"I don't change diapers," Daddy said handing her to me, and taking the spatula. I took her into the powder room and laid her on the floor.

"Boo-boo!" she said patting her fat diaper.

"Move your hands, nasty girl," I said. I could hardly wait until she was old enough to sleep in panties at night.

Daddy had hired managers to run both the restaurants. One was only opened for lunch and dinner. That was the one in
188

downtown Brooklyn. The one on the corner was opened for breakfast, lunch and dinner.

"What are we going to do today?" I asked Mommy.

"Your father and I have a surprise for you," Mommy answered winking her eye at Daddy.

We went to look at the brownstones that were being remodeled.

"Brian wants to rent an apartment in this one. I thought I would let him have it for three-hundred dollars a month. This building has three apartments in it, and the basement apartment. We're still having some problems with water damage down there and we're trying to figure out where it's coming from. I told him he could have one of the apartments on the top floor. It has an attic that can be turned into a room, if he decides to get it. Can you watch the kids, honey while I show her the top floor?" Daddy asked Mommy.

He and I went up to the top floor apartment. It was gorgeous. The detailing on the wood was amazing. There were built-in bookshelves in the attic and a huge round window that had a view of the downtown skyline.

"If he doesn't want it, I'll take it," I said.

"I've got something better for you," Daddy said.

We went next door to the other building. The remodeling work on it was complete. When we stepped into the beautiful ceramic tiled foyer with an Italian chandelier overhead, I knew that this was where I needed to be. I put Marissa down so she

189

could run through the house. Daddy gave me a tour of my new home.

"It is absolutely gorgeous, Daddy," I cried, hugging him tightly.

That night I tried to reach Michael again. He wasn't home nor did the answering machine come on. He was really getting on my nerves. I hung up and called Leon.

"How's my lady?" he asked when he heard my voice.

"I'm doing great now that I hear your voice," I said. I told Leon about the brownstone my father had gotten for me. I told him about the nightclub and restaurant that I was looking at getting if the price was right. I was so excited, and Leon shared my excitement with me. We talked over an hour again that night.

When I sat down in the den with Mommy after the babies were bathed and put to bed, the phone rang. It was Michael.

"I found the perfect place to open my business. It's right around the corner from my Dad's restaurant," I said.

"Do you really think that desert experience you have is enough for you to run a real club?" he asked.

"I ran a real club for four years," I said annoyed.

"If that's what you want to call it," he said.

"Excuse me! Do I hear some jealousy in your voice because I am doing exactly what I wanted to do when I got out of school and you're no closer to being a dentist than you were ten years

190

ago," I snapped. I slammed the phone down so hard I thought I had broken it.

"Why do you even bother to call him?" Mommy asked, passing me a bowl of popcorn and a wine cooler.

The next day with Travis strapped to the front of me and Daddy pushing Marissa in the stroller, we met the owners of the club at two in the afternoon. We walked in and it was as if my dream was laid out before me. This was exactly what I had pictured. I tried not to let my excitement show as we walked into the restaurant. There were some things that I would definitely want to change, but they were all minor things. I had to have this building. I just had to!

We told the owners that we needed to think about it and we would get back with them in twenty-four hours. We stepped out into the bright sunshine and calmly walked around the corner and jumped up and down.

"This is you, baby!" Daddy said excitedly.

It sure was! The next day we sealed the deal and started the ball rolling. I didn't even bother to waste my time calling Michael. I wanted a divorce. Moreover, I wanted to get it before he got out of the service. I wanted it yesterday!

The babies and I went to our new house alone. I spread out a blanket on the hardwood floor and sat down beside Marissa. I sat Travis down in front of me and we watched Marissa as she went straight to the fireplace.

191

"Hey, handsome," I said to him. He smiled widely, revealing a tooth coming in. He was only six months old. "Hey boy where did you get that tooth?"

I laughed tickling him. He was so fat and lovable. He laughed and rolled away from me. We were going to be just fine. We didn't need Michael. He was a thorn in my side anyway. I had reached a point where everything that he did bothered me. The sound of him breathing drove me crazy. It was best to move on.

On Sunday morning, Mommy and I were in the kitchen making breakfast and Daddy was reading the paper. The doorbell rang at ten sharp, just as the clock was chiming. I could hear Daddy talking to someone, but couldn't hear anyone saying anything. He stood in the doorway, a solemn look on his face.

"What is it, Clyde?" Mommy asked.

"It's Michael. He was in a car accident this morning and was killed," he said. I closed the cabinet and turned to face him.

"What?" I asked.

"Michael's dead," he said softly.

I sat down at the table and Mommy gasped.

"What happened to him?" I asked.

"He was in a car accident, Toni," he said. I had heard him say it, but it seemed so surreal.

"I'll call the Red Cross," he said.

192

"Have some coffee, baby," Mommy said.

The next few days were a blur. I know that Daddy and Brian flew to New Mexico to get Michael's body and to make sure that our personal belongings would be shipped to us. Aunt Wezie had been hanging around the house for the past couple days. At first, I didn't mind because she was helping Mommy arrange for the funeral. Now she was always talking about something negative.

"That nigger wasn't about nothing any way. God don't like ugly. Its karma," she said a hundred times a day. I didn't want to hear it so I stayed in my bedroom with the door closed.

"He took my niece out there in that desert and treated her like she was nothing! He messed around on her and got another woman pregnant. He ought to be glad that he had a woman like Antoinette. No good dog! He can't even deny this baby. He looks just like his big-eyed self. I didn't like him no how. Never did. He was shifty," she said.

"Louise, nobody wants to hear that mess today. Just cut up the greens and shut up!" Mommy snapped. Neither of them had noticed me standing in the doorway. I went back upstairs to lie down.

I called Leon. "Has anyone told you about the newspaper article?" he asked.

"No, what is it about?" I asked.

"It said he was engaged to be married to the woman that was killed with him," he told me.

193

"A woman was killed with him?" I asked shocked.

"Nobody told you?" he asked surprised.

"No," I said.

"Do you want me to read you the article?" he asked.

"Yeah, read it to me," I said.

"An Air Force Sergeant and his fiancé were killed by a drunk driver on Sunday in San Antonio, Texas. Staff Sergeant Michael B. Robinson and Sergeant Felicia Marie Pierce were returning from a concert in Dallas when the car they were driving was hit head on by a pickup truck driven by forty-five year old Daniel Morrow of Dallas. Morrow crossed the median and hit them head on, killing them instantly. Morrow's blood alcohol level was .18," Leon said.

"That's enough. I don't want to hear the rest," I said interrupting him.

"Are you okay?" he asked.

"Yeah, I filed for a divorce a couple days ago. We didn't even get a chance to do the final paper work on it. I hadn't even told him that I wanted a divorce and he's already engaged?" I said.

"Toni, I don't know what to say that will make this better for you," he said.

I didn't think that there was anything that anyone could say. This was the final chapter of my marriage to Michael. After the funeral, that would be it. No more drama.

When Daddy returned home, he was very quiet. He hadn't told me that a woman had been in the car yet, and I was sure that it was eating him up trying to decide if he should mention it or not. I decided to make it easier for him. I let him know that I knew.

"I'm really disappointed in Michael. I thought he had his act together after this affair with that other woman. But he didn't learn a damn thing! We're not going to waste a lot of time with this thing. Okay. We'll have the funeral and lay him to rest, and move on. You have these babies to look after and your mother and I will be right here to help you in any way we can. We've never wallowed in mess, and we ain't going to start now. Okay?" he said.

"Okay," I agreed.

We made the funeral arrangements. We made sure that he was in his dress blues, and that the Air Force would pay for his burial. I checked with the insurance company and sent them a copy of the death certificate. The policy I had him in had a clause for accidental death. I expected to get a check for one-half million dollars in a couple of weeks. In the meantime, we had a funeral to go to.

I took my seat in the family car alongside Brian, Mommy, Daddy and the babies. We drove in silence to the graveyard. Travis was very restless that day. I passed him to Daddy to hold. Mommy clutched my hand and Brian allowed me to rest my head on his shoulder.

When we arrived at the graveyard the soldiers were there that would perform the twenty one gun salute. I dreaded that part of the ceremony the most. I had taken a valium before I left the house, but I was so wired up it hadn't done what it was supposed to do. The minister read a couple of scriptures from the Bible and we prayed. As soon as he had said Amen, I stood to go to the car. I wasn't going to be able to sit through anything else. My heels sank into the damp earth as I made my way back to the car.

"I believe that she done lost her mind. Look at her. Where is she going?" Aunt Wezie asked.

I just shook my head and kept walking. The driver opened the door for me and I slid across the cold leather seats and shut my eyes.

The house was full of members of Michael's family. Tina was also there with Remy. He was fourteen years old now. As far as I knew, he hadn't heard from Michael in years. I had sent his mom a money order every month for $300 at first and as we made more money, I increased it to $400. I sent cards for his birthday and other holidays.

"Hi Tina," I said.

"Hello. How are you?" she asked.

"I'm fine. What about you?" I asked. I didn't really care how she was doing. I *did* care about Remy. He looked lost and sad. "Would you like to meet your little sister and brother?" I asked him. I held out my hand to him when he nodded yes. I took him up stairs where Marissa was lying across the bed sleeping. When I laid her down, she was fully dressed. Now she was wearing only her slip, one sock and no panties. Travis was playing in his crib.

"Hey, little man. How are you doing?" I asked him as he pulled himself up and laughed loudly. I took him out of the crib and handed him to Remy. "This is Travis," I said. Remy was nervous and walked to the bed and sat down. Travis put his hand to Remy's mouth. I guessed the braces caught his eye.

"He's cute," Remy said

"What grade are you in now?" I asked.

"I'm in the tenth grade. I got put up a grade because I'm smart, I guess," he said, smiling.

"Oh, really? What do you like to do for recreation?" I asked.

"I like to play basketball and I like roller skating," he answered.

I walked him back downstairs and thanked his mother for bringing him over. I gave them my address and phone number. When I looked for him an hour later, they had left. I made a mental note to set some of the insurance money aside for his college education and his support right now.

I wanted everyone to leave, but they hadn't had a chance to eat yet. The living room, den and dining room was full of people. I went into the kitchen to hear Aunt Wezie entertaining everyone there. She had pushed the babies' high chairs together and was feeding them chicken, rice, and some string beans.

"Look at 'em. They could past for twins. Ain't no way he could have denied this baby. I would have left his sorry behind years ago," she said to anyone that would listen to her.

I went into the kitchen where Daddy was carving a ham. I got a biscuit, put a piece of meat on it, and grabbed a bottle of Scotch from the cabinet. I went back upstairs, not even speaking to anyone.

I turned on the television and watched a rerun of Dallas while I sipped from the bottle of Scotch and ate my biscuit. I must have fallen asleep for a while because when I woke up and went downstairs, everyone was gone. Daddy was lying on the couch watching television while Travis slept in his arms. Marissa was in the playpen sleeping.

"Where's Mommy?" I asked.

"I think she's in the kitchen cleaning up," he said.

She had already washed up all of the dishes and was tying up a bag of garbage.

"I'll take that out for you," I said. She kissed me on the cheek.

"How are you doing?" she asked. I hugged her tightly. I wanted to scream. I wanted to cry. I had done neither. I had been fighting it, but I felt like I was going to break down any minute. I knew Daddy would be disappointed if he saw me crying. Mommy and I sat in the kitchen talking about the funeral.

"Honey, don't be upset with your Aunt Wezie. She really doesn't mean any harm. She just doesn't know what to say most of the time. If she would just think first, she might be okay, huh?" Mommy said.

"I know she don't mean to be insensitive, but that is exactly what she comes across as. I don't even know if she knows how to stop and think before she opens up and lets it rip," I said.

"Michael looked good. They had fixed him up very nicely. He just had that little cut across his eyebrow," she said.

"I didn't even look at him," I told her.

"You didn't? Why?" she asked.

"I just wanted to remember him how I saw him the last time. Besides, you know I don't like funerals and stuff," I said.

"Toni, have you cried?" she asked.

"No, Mommy. I keep fighting it. But, I am about to crack." I confided.

"Baby, let me tell you something. Michael was your first love. You've been with him since you were sixteen years old. That's what, ten or eleven years? You loved him. He was your husband. Don't you dare not mourn the death of your husband because you're afraid of what your father will say. You are a widow at twenty-seven years old. You have two children that you now have to take care of alone. You were ending your marriage, yes, but you did not expect Michael to die. So, this is your party, and you can cry if you want to," she said.

She fixed me a plate of food and we sat talking some more. On that Thursday, the kids and I were scheduled to move into our brownstone and Brian was moving into his apartment. It appeared as if my life was going on, however each night I lay in bed crying myself to sleep and clutching a bottle of scotch. I was alone and so very scared. I kept up appearances because "we didn't waste a lot of time wallowing in mess."

I remembered when I was five years old and my mother left us alone and how I just wanted to cry and scream, but my father told me I could only cry one night about her leaving. The next day life continued and I cried silently while this awful fire burned in my chest. I couldn't go through that again. I was a woman now, an adult with a family of my own. I didn't want my children to think that there was something wrong with hurting and showing that hurt. I was going to crack up if I didn't do something. Though I talked to Leon every night, he wasn't here, and I needed him to be here. He had already processed out and was just waiting to be released from duty. I could hardly wait for him to come and see about me.

So much was going on in my life. The restaurant needed new ovens, so they were being installed. Between making sure that the moving men didn't break up my furniture, I had to also make sure that the contractors did what they were supposed to do at the restaurant. I was having the walls painted and new covers put on the seats in the club. I was also in negotiations with Roger Troutman and Zapp to be my opening act. Travis was trying to walk, and he had two more teeth coming in, so he was grouchy. Marissa was all over the place, getting into all kinds of mischief. I was also trying to keep my relationship with Leon on the down low because I didn't want to start folks gossiping; but I was aching to be with him.

THROUGH THE FIRE

Every morning at eight, Daddy showed up so that we could get our day started. He didn't know that I hadn't even been to sleep or that I had drank a fifth of scotch the night before. I would take a nice hot shower and put on makeup to cover up the bags under my eyes. I curled my hair and got dressed before I got the babies up. I packed up diaper bags with pampers, bottles of juice, Tupperware containers of homemade baby food for Travis, and snack foods and toys and extra clothing for them both. Both of the babies were early birds, so they were up, bathed and dressed by seven-thirty. When Daddy came for us, we were ready.

It had been almost three months and I hadn't gotten more than three hours of sleep each night. I had lost about fifteen pounds and I felt awful, but I smiled and laughed and acted like everything was just fine. Unfortunately, I couldn't keep it up for long.

One morning I met Daddy at the door still in my pajamas. My hair was all over my head. It took everything that I had to even come down the stairs and get the door.

"What's up baby girl?" he asked happily.

Daddy, can you take the babies to your house and keep them for me until tomorrow? I am struggling, Daddy. I want to scream! I can't take this acting like nothing has happened. My world has changed drastically and I am about to go crazy. I just need one day to cry. Just one day. Tomorrow, I'll be fine. Take the babies, please Daddy," I begged.

We dressed them quickly and I walked with him downstairs. At the door, he turned to me, "Toni, I love you. You cry and whatever you want to do. You also need to pray. Pray to Jehovah and he will answer you. Your Momma will tell you," he said.

He kissed me and left. I went to the kitchen, put a bagel in the toaster oven, and poured a glass of juice. I don't know when I had eaten it had been so long.

CHAPTER 25

JUST AS I WAS ABOUT TO GO back upstairs the doorbell rang. I went to the door and through the paned glass; I could see Mommy standing there. I opened the door and let her in. She was carrying a cardboard box that was taped up tightly. She kissed me on the cheek and stepped inside.

"I've been cleaning up the attic and I found this box. It has your name on it and a date. August 9, 1967. I thought you might want to see what is in it," she said. She carried it into the kitchen and sat it on the table.

I poured us a cup of coffee and we went into the living room setting the box in the floor between us. I pulled the tape off the box and opened the flaps.

There was a picture of me taken when I was in the first grade. I smiled showing two missing teeth and two Shirley Temple curled ponytails. I handed the picture to Mommy, who laughed loudly when she saw it. There was a small photo album. I opened. There was a picture of me and CJ taken when we lived in Harlem. Neither of us had on shirts, and we looked like those children you see on television that are starving. Every one of our ribs showed. I laughed, wiping a tear from my eyes. There was CJ tied in a chair eating a bowl of oatmeal. He was covered from his forehead down to his toes in oatmeal. Poor CJ!

203

The tears were coming faster now. I turned the next page and saw a picture of my birth mother, wearing a black slip, and putting on makeup to go out and party. Her hair was cut short on one side and long on the other. The track marks were visible in this picture. That wasn't what caught my eye, though. Her smile was erotic. Daddy took this picture and the way she was looking into the camera lens was hauntingly sensual. I turned the page to see the next picture of me and her. I was sitting in the floor between her legs getting my hair braided. My face couldn't be seen, but she was again looking into the camera lens. I had never seen anyone look that intense before. I handed the book to Mommy and picked up a small dress that I probably wore when I was little. It smelled so familiar. I held it to my face and took a deep breath. The dress was pink with layers of crinoline under it. It had a big bow in the back and a wide lacy collar. I didn't ever remember wearing it. I laid it on the floor and there was my brown teddy bear. I picked it up and held it to my chest. Oh my goodness! It was missing an eye, and was torn under his right arm. Blood stains were on his feet. That happened the night that my birth mother had stabbed Daddy. I just held it to me and bawled like a baby remembering that scene.

I will never forget the look of horror on Daddy's face when he realized that he had been stabbed. He looked at me for a pregnant moment, no doubt wondering if he would be around to see me grow up before he fell to the floor in a bloody heap. Mommy put her arms around me and held me while I cried.

"These are memories from a different time in your life. But, you should know where you came from in order to go forward in your life. I truly wish that I could kiss it and make it all better for you baby. Toni, I think that you should try to find Carol Ann, your birth mother. You're older, she's older. I think that you should find her, get it settled in here," Mommy said pointing to my heart. She held me and caressed my cheek. I couldn't have asked a better person to be in my life. I was truly blessed having her.

The doorbell rang suddenly.

"I've got another surprise for you," Mommy said getting up from the floor and going to the door. I picked up our coffee cups and took them into kitchen. As I turned the corner, there stood Leon smiling so beautifully. I ran into his opened arms and held him tightly.

"I told you if it was meant to be, we would be together!" he said, holding me tightly.

THE END